Shay leaned forward over the seat between them. "Granger?"

He didn't look back at her. "The plane's been tampered with," he said. "I've lost all my fuel."

Tampered with? Vianni? How did they know...? "How? Damn it, Granger. How?"

Granger swore, flipping dials and gripping whatever parts of the plane steered the dang thing. He didn't answer her question, and she understood why. The plane was making terrible grinding noises, and he was doing everything to stop them.

Shay didn't demand anything else. She didn't even watch him work—she knew nothing about planes. Instead, she did something she hadn't done since she was a little girl, and maybe once when she'd pulled Granger's lifeless body out of that burning building two years ago.

She prayed, quietly to herself as things coughed and screeched and jangled. A cacophony of noises that had her stomach twisting in terrible, terrified knots.

But what came next was so much worse.

Silence. Nothing but absolute silence.

UNDERCOVER RESCUE

NICOLE HELM

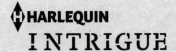
HARLEQUIN

INTRIGUE

For everyone who waited so patiently for Shay's story.

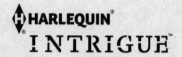

ISBN-13: 978-1-335-48964-7

Undercover Rescue

Copyright © 2022 by Nicole Helm

Harlequin Enterprises ULC
22 Adelaide St. West, 41st Floor
Toronto, Ontario M5H 4E3, Canada
www.Harlequin.com

Printed in U.S.A.

Nicole Helm grew up with her nose in a book and the dream of one day becoming a writer. Luckily, after a few failed career choices, she gets to follow that dream—writing down-to-earth contemporary romance and romantic suspense. From farmers to cowboys, Midwest to the West, Nicole writes stories about people finding themselves and finding love in the process. She lives in Missouri with her husband and two sons and dreams of someday owning a barn.

Books by Nicole Helm

Harlequin Intrigue

A North Star Novel Series

Summer Stalker
Shot Through the Heart
Mountainside Murder
Cowboy in the Crosshairs
Dodging Bullets in Blue Valley
Undercover Rescue

A Badlands Cops Novel

South Dakota Showdown
Covert Complication
Backcountry Escape
Isolated Threat
Badlands Beware
Close Range Christmas

Carsons & Delaneys: Battle Tested

Wyoming Cowboy Marine
Wyoming Cowboy Sniper
Wyoming Cowboy Ranger
Wyoming Cowboy Bodyguard

Visit the Author Profile page at Harlequin.com.

CAST OF CHARACTERS

Veronica Shay—Current head of North Star. Has been hiding her past from everyone, except Granger, her entire decade with North Star, but now it's coming out.

Granger Macmillan—Former head of North Star and current hermit rancher. Helps North Star occasionally with missions. Knew Shay before he started North Star, back in Chicago, when he was a DEA agent and she married into a Mafia family.

Frankie Vianni—Head of a Mafia family who was once married to Shay. Was supposed to be dead but now wants revenge against both her and Granger, since he was instrumental in taking down Frankie's family before he rebuilt it.

Wyatt brothers—Cody, Jamison and Tucker all worked with Shay at some point in her North Star career and come back to North Star to help save Shay, since she once helped them.

Current and former North Star agents—Reece, Holden, Sabrina, Conner, Froggy, Elsie, Betty, Mallory, Gabriel and Zeke all work together to help Shay when they find out she and Granger are in trouble.

Anna Vianni-Macmillan—Granger's late wife, who was also Shay's sister-in-law when she married Frankie.

Chapter One

Veronica Shay—or Veronica Vianni, depending on what legal document a person went by—had grown up knowing how to lie. She'd had a natural aptitude for it, much to her parents' dismay. She'd courted the wrong side of the law until they'd disowned her.

She hadn't cared much at the time. After all, she'd found her own family. A place she belonged.

Or so it had seemed.

It hadn't been a happily-ever-after, and for years she'd blamed everyone else for the horror she'd gotten herself into. It had only been when she'd started to take responsibility for her own actions that things had started to change.

She packed her bag *now*, trying not to think too deeply about *then*. The way her life had changed. So much for the better. She'd turned herself into someone who did the right thing. Who took down the bad guys rather than glittered on their arm.

Shay, the head of the North Star Group, a secretive collection of skilled operatives who'd worked

together to take down the vicious Sons of the Badlands gang, and then thwarted a dangerous death
machine supplying military grade weapons to all
the wrong people, wasn't remotely recognizable to
the eighteen-year-old Veronica Shay who'd married
Frankie Vianni fifteen years ago.

Frankie Vianni who was supposed to be dead,
but clearly *wasn't*. And thus was a threat to every
member of North Star. Because there was no way
he'd forgiven and forgotten the way she'd gotten out
of the Vianni Mafia family—by getting a fat lot of
them killed or jailed.

Shay hadn't expected to escape unscathed. Even
when Granger Macmillan had taken her under his
wing and brought her in on the ground floor of starting the North Star Group, she'd been waiting for
Frankie to appear.

Two years ago, he or the ghost of him had nearly
killed Granger, and because of pure luck or skill it
was only *nearly*.

But someone had been irrevocably hurt, and it
hadn't been her. The cause for it all. It had a member of her North Star family.

She wouldn't let that happen again. No matter
what she had to do. Frankie had made it clear he was
making his move. So, Shay would move right back.
She would act. Bullet wound or no bullet wound.

She'd finally gotten rid of Betty, one of her closest
friends and North Star's doctor. Sent her off to Mon-
tana to start her new life, and thus be out of Shay's

hair. Sabrina and Connor were still around, two of her lead field agents, but she'd put them in charge of a mission that had gotten a few other regulars out of North Star headquarters.

She'd hired a pilot who wouldn't ask questions, asked him to meet her at an off-grid air strip, and was prepared to deal with her past, rather than wait for it to deal with her.

Because even if the past few weeks had been calm as she'd healed, she knew it wasn't over. Frankie was just trying to make her sweat.

He didn't know the woman she'd become.

Shay slung her bag over her shoulder and winced. In an ideal world, she wouldn't be this hurt or in this much pain, but she'd made her choice to leave ideal behind a long time ago.

She left her room. She didn't *sneak*—sneaking would make someone pay too much attention, if someone did in fact see her. Which she had planned around.

She'd created this North Star headquarters. After their old one had burned down, thanks in part to Frankie's family, and Granger had put her in charge, she'd moved them from South Dakota to Wyoming. She'd designed this compound on an old deserted ranch, and worked hard to lead North Star as they took down people doing bad in the world.

This year had been successful and yet, important pieces of her team had left North Star for a real life. Marriage and babies and futures somewhere else.

Not risking their lives. *Not* constantly fighting the bad in the world.

Once upon a time, Shay wouldn't have understood it. She would have scoffed at it, in fact. But her life had changed since that explosion over two years ago. Was it an age thing? Was it the fact that the man most hurt in the explosion was her one and only tie to her past?

She didn't know. So much so, she wasn't fully sure who she was anymore. She didn't even know what she wanted.

Except to be free of her youthful mistakes without them touching anyone else she cared about.

Shay walked with all the authority she could muster as she moved through the maze of hallways and then out the front door.

Easy as you please. She slid her sunglasses on her face against the blinding sun bouncing off the snow. The vehicle would be a bit trickier. Since it was North Star property, any of their tech people could have it tracked.

She still hadn't figured out this part yet. Her best bet was to take a car and ditch it somewhere. Probably in the opposite direction of the airstrip.

No one was going to let her disappear. She'd tried that already. But Vianni's men had been on her tail so she hadn't had a chance to get everything in order first. And North Star had stepped in and stopped Vianni's men.

But Frankie hadn't been there. Likely, he'd sent a

group of volunteers just to see if they could breech North Star. He wouldn't risk his own life until it was a sure thing.

Shay wasn't about to let it be a sure thing. She wasn't about to let her friends, or more accurately *found family* in North Star, step in and get hurt in the process. This wasn't North Star business. This was *Veronica Shay* business—an identity no one in her current life knew existed.

Except Granger Macmillan and Nina Wyatt. Nina wouldn't tell. In the year Nina had known about Shay's past, she'd never told her husband, which meant she'd snitch to no one.

Granger… Well, he was a bit more of a wild card these days but since his past connected to hers, she doubted he was in a hurry to let anyone in on it.

So, she got in her North Star vehicle and drove into Wanayi, a small town where Shay often went to buy groceries or other necessities. She studied the vehicles in the gas station parking lot. Any would be easy enough to steal, but none of them looked like they belonged to people who'd have an easy time replacing them.

She sat in her car, parked in the far corner of the lot, keeping out of sight, watching the comings and goings trying to figure out how to accomplish her goal. After about thirty minutes of this, a cab drove into the parking lot.

As far as signs went, Shay was willing to take this one. She watched the driver gas up, head inside.

While he was paying, she quickly moved across the lot and slid into the back seat.

Even cabbies didn't lock up out here.

When he returned, he eyed her through the window before getting in. If he was surprised to find someone sitting in his cab, he didn't act it. But when he slid into the driver's side, he didn't close the door. He kept it open and one leg out.

"I'm off duty. No money on me," the man said in a smoker's rasp.

Shay held two twenties over the seats. "I've got cash. Half now. Half at the drop-off point. All you have to do is drive and not ask any questions and you can pocket that cash."

The man eyed the money, then his phone sitting in the middle console. Shay figured he was considering calling the cops. She couldn't blame him. She'd even let him—once she got the hell out of Dodge.

Eventually he took the bills and slid them into his pocket. He pulled his leg into the car and asked for an address. Shay gave him one in the general direction of where she was going.

He drove, eyeing her in the rearview every so often. She kept herself looking relaxed, her bag far enough out of reach that he didn't think she'd grab it and try something shady.

When he got close enough to the airfield she thought she could walk without hurting her injuries too much, she leaned slowly forward. "This'll do."

The cabbie slowed to a stop, eyeing her suspiciously. "This ain't nowhere."

"Exactly." Shay handed him a hundred-dollar bill, didn't hurt to sweeten the pot. "Not a soul needs to know. Got it?"

He studied the bill, then her, and shrugged. "Fine."

She didn't know if it'd be enough. Especially if someone questioned him, but it would give her a head start anyway.

Shay got out of the cab, looked around. The snow would slow her down, but it was sunny day which would keep the bitter cold at bay. She didn't look back at the cab driver. Instead, she just got to work.

She walked away from the highway. Best not to be spotted if any car passed by. She knew the area well enough, because she'd studied it when she'd chosen North Star. Before they'd gotten their own little airstrip, they'd used this one.

It was about a mile. Not long, but she was dragging. Too damn tired for a little hike. This gunshot wound was a real pain.

Finally, she reached the private airstrip. Just a long strip of earth in the middle of nowhere. A plane was parked by the tiny office building.

She didn't head for the building. If she could avoid that, and just get to the pilot, she'd be better off. She frowned at the plane as she got closer. There was something vaguely familiar about it. Then again, all planes looked the same to her. Especially these small single engine ones that looked more like they belonged in an old WWII movie.

She didn't see any evidence of a pilot, so she moved for the plane. As she got closer, she could make out a pair of boots next to the opposite wheel. So someone was standing on the other side of the plane, most likely refueling or something.

Still, Shay surreptitiously put her hand close to the gun she had concealed at her back.

When the body stepped around, she braced herself for a fight. A nasty surprise.

The man's face was a surprise, but not quite the one she was expecting.

Tall, broad and all too familiar, even if she hadn't seen that reckless smile of his in too many years to name. Not because he'd been such a stranger, but because he hadn't smiled much since his injuries two years ago.

"Where to?" he asked.

Shay looked at him and knew she had three options.

She went with the dumb one, simply because it would feel good. She threw a punch.

"I'LL GIVE YOU that one for free," Granger Macmillan said, forcing himself to smile though he didn't feel it. Not because the blow had been painful, but because it hadn't been. He'd trained Shay himself. She was usually a better punch. Which meant her wound was really slowing her down.

"You don't give anyone anything for free, Granger," she grumbled.

He might have argued with her, but since she was the only one he made allowances for these days, it felt a little too close to a truth he didn't want to parse.

"You look ridiculous in that hat," she said distastefully. "You're no cowboy."

"I don't know." He adjusted the hat on his head. "I think the cowboy life is growing on me."

She rolled her eyes.

"But I'd never give up flying." He patted the plane's glossy wing. "So, why don't you hop in and we can head off? Time's a wasting."

"So strange I don't recall inviting you."

He kept his voice as even as hers, without the casually cutting edge to it. "Well, good thing I don't need an invitation then."

She blew out a breath, clearly trying to get a hold of her temper. The problem she was going to run into was that he knew her better than anyone—including Betty or Nina or anyone else she considered her closest friends.

Because Granger had known her *before*. Had been the hand held out to save her from the Vianni family, and he knew for a fact not one person in their current lives knew what she'd been through or what she'd done before she'd turned herself into Shay, North Star operative and eventual leader.

He knew what people had thought back when he'd been in charge of North Star and given Shay more freedom and leeway than he'd given any of his other agents. That there'd been more going on between them than met the eye.

It had bothered him, but he'd always figured the best way to fight that rumor was to keep his hands to himself and his focus on the only thing North Star had been about back then: bringing down the Sons of the Badlands.

The gang had been instrumental in the murder of his wife, but only because the Vianni family had let them be.

"This has nothing to do with you," Shay said.

His attempt at keeping his cool faded. Maybe it was the memory of Anna's death, or maybe he was just tired of constantly being haunted by a past he couldn't seem to escape no matter how hard he tried. "The hell it doesn't."

"They were after me. They shot *me*." She didn't look him in the eye when she said either of those things, so she had to know.

"I heard they were asking about me too."

Her gaze whipped up to meet his. A storm in those blue depths. Not unusual—Shay had always been something of a storm. But this one wasn't controlled the way it needed to be if they were going to beat Vianni.

"It was a distraction," she said firmly.

If he was someone else, he might have even believed her. "How do you know?"

"Why would Frankie care about you, Granger?"

"I was married to his sister. I'm not the uncon-nected piece you want to make me."

"Anna's dead."

Yes, she was. It had taken him a long time—too long—to really accept that. To finally grieve and let go. Maybe it was only now that he was even getting there, but if he could count himself truly healed that meant every mention of her couldn't put his back up. "Yes, Anna's dead. How does he know you're not? *We're* not?"

"I don't know. I intend to find out."

"You need a pilot." He pointed at himself.

"Yeah, one who'll drop me off and let me do what I need to do. Not play babysitter and try to make this about him and his dead wife."

A barb she knew would land, and God help him, he couldn't quite fight it off. "Get in the plane, Shay. Before I make you."

She raised an eyebrow at him.

"You aren't yourself. You're injured and still re-covering. You need help. Now, you can pretend like you don't, but it's only going to get you killed be-fore you even land." He held up a hand. "And before you argue with me, understand that punch didn't even hurt. I damn well wish it had, but it didn't. You hiked, what, a mile? And could barely catch your breath. I've been where you are, Shay. I know how much it weakens you. You need someone. If it's not going to be me, pick your poison. But someone."

She stood there, utterly still. Granger did the

same, and he worked hard to keep his shoulders re-laxed, to breathe instead of hold his breath. Why wouldn't she choose someone else? That Lindstrom guy she'd brought into North Star a few months ago could fly well enough, and was big and capable of handling whatever Shay waded into.

But this was about Vianni. It was about all they'd escaped ten years ago. It was about *their* pasts.

"What about your dogs?" she asked.

"I took them out to Reece's place."

She eventually let the bag slide off her shoulder and land with a thump on the ground. "I'm not going to Chicago," she said, strain evident in her voice.

"I didn't say you were." He grabbed her bag and tossed it in the plane. "You're going to the Vianni compound in Idaho. The one you've been researching for two years, and just found the exact coordinates to…what was it? Thursday?"

She didn't look surprised that he knew it. Just re-signed. *Tired.*

"I'll let you fly me there, but you'll stay back. Let me handle this my way. I'll call in backup if I need it, but—"

"No," Granger said firmly, warring with his own temper and impatience. "We do this together."

"I get that you think because of Anna you have some connection to all this. But this is about me and Frankie. You're a pawn, maybe. Just like Anna was in the end. Don't fall for it twice, Granger."

"We do this together," he repeated. "That's the

beginning and end of it. You can be pissy about it, bring Anna up as much as you want, but it doesn't change a damn thing. Vianni knows who and what we are and have been, and we need to stop whoever is left of that family before anyone else we care about is put in danger. Nothing else matters. Not your pride. Not your fears. That's what got you shot."

She quirked a brow. "Oh, is that what got me shot?"

"Yeah, it is. I know. I've been there. Remember? You're lucky they didn't get those explosives off like they did when they tried to take me out. You'd be dead."

"You weren't."

"Close enough." In more ways than one. "Get in the plane, Shay. And on the way, get used to the fact that we're partners now. Full stop."

Chapter Two

Shay got in the plane because she was tired. She got in the plane because it was there and once she got to Idaho, she'd ditch Granger.

She kept insisting in her own brain she'd leave him in the dust. Kept trying to convince herself she would and could.

But somewhere high in the clouds with the white of a Wyoming winter stretching out below them in this tiny old plane, Shay accepted the fact that in this *one* moment, Granger was right.

They had to be in this together. That was the fate she'd handcuffed herself to when she'd allowed him to give her a way out of her life and inevitable death in the Vianni family.

Maybe she'd known that all along. Maybe that was why she'd been so bound and determined to do it herself.

Allowing Granger into anything always made her life ten times more complicated. But life *was* complicated. Especially when you had a well of mistakes to atone for.

So, she worked on accepting her fate. In the cold and the loud rumble of the engine vibrating her from the inside out. They would work together. Put the Vianni ghosts to bed and then…

She closed her eyes against the wave of emotion that threatened. That had been threatening for months now.

She'd held on for two years, leading North Star through taking out the rest of the Sons of the Badlands. Finding new missions. Keeping everyone together and whole and working for *good*.

But Reece Montgomery, her lead field agent and most senior agent, had left this summer. Hard and cold Reece had fallen in *love*. And something about that had fractured…everything.

Seeing him with his pregnant wife, his stepson and lately the new baby, Shay had begun to realize that all these years she'd been trying to *do* something good, she'd mostly been running away from all the bad she'd done. And all the things she didn't know about herself. And sometimes even what she did know.

Like she didn't like being head of North Star. She didn't want to be an administrator or puppeteer or whatever it was she was supposed to have been. And worse, so much worse, she didn't want to be a field agent anymore. She didn't want to go back to the grind, the deception, the fighting. Once, that had been her entire life, but she felt creaky and old now.

Veronica Shay wanted to rest. She wanted some kind of…life. Like all the people who'd become her family were finding and building.

She didn't deserve it, but God she wanted it.

Sighing, she studied the man in the pilot's seat in front of her.

She'd known him, or at least of him, since she was seventeen. Frankie had put *Veronica* on his arm for all his fancy parties, showed her off like the decoration that she didn't realize she was and pointed out Granger Macmillan to her.

That man is the enemy, Veronica. Never forget, he wants us and our kind dead.

She'd asked him why they didn't just kill him then. She'd meant it. Frankie was the grandson of a group of dirty cops who'd been exposed and arrested, but the rest of the family had come together to build Vianni part two. They didn't even pretend to be law enforcement this time around. They were a mob family. Plain and simple.

They could have taken out some lowly DEA agent, Veronica had been sure of it. Had been intrigued by the power Frankie so often claimed to have.

Frankie had given her a cold smile and told her it was complicated.

Boy, had it been complicated.

Still was, though in different ways than it had been. And now, as Granger began their descent, Shay accepted that they were going to do this together. Because he was right, even if Frankie wasn't after Granger, they both had Vianni ghosts that needed to be laid to rest.

And Shay was not at her normal fighting shape. It would be smart to lean on Granger. Who knew… who understood.

She just wished it was *anyone else*.

He landed on another isolated strip of land. With a similar setup to the last one. Small building and hangar. This one wasn't as deserted though. A short rotund man exited the office as they touched ground.

Granger got out, then helped her out of the plane. She was beyond irritated she needed the help.

"Russ," Granger said, nodding to the man staring at them.

"Mac. Gas her up?"

Granger nodded. "I'll be back in a day or two, but feel free to bill me for the week."

"Got it."

Granger ushered her away from the office and toward a small parking lot that had a few cars and trucks parked in it. Granger pulled keys out of his pocket and the small nondescript sedan's lights flashed. "That's mine."

Shay nodded and didn't ask questions about how he had a car here already, if only because she knew he expected her to. She might be working with him on this, but that didn't mean she had to give him what he expected. She was too tired to play mental gymnastics with him, and she hurt all over.

She needed a nap, a meal and her pain meds.

They got into the car and Granger began to drive like he knew exactly where he was headed. Shay had no doubt he did. That's what this man did. Made plans. Plotted. Accomplished.

That was who he was at his core. So in control. She'd once had an uncomfortable hero worship toward him. He'd saved her, given her a purpose. He'd plotted and planned and taken down the group that had killed his wife, the group that had partnered with the Vianni family to do more widespread damage.

She'd felt betrayed when his need for revenge had somewhat overshadowed the good they were doing with North Star. She'd grown disillusioned enough to bend his rules, to stand up to him. But she'd never left. She'd never fully killed that part of her that felt like she owed him.

Then everything had blown up—literally and figuratively. And she still hadn't forgiven him for leaving North Star the way he had. Something she hadn't fully admitted to herself until this moment.

She'd called him in on a few missions lately because he'd been physically recovered. Because he was always in the wings. But their relationship had changed. Soured. There was an antagonism that had grown, not leveled out, since the explosion.

She'd convinced herself it was power plays and Granger not being able to see her as a leader even though he'd put her in that position, but part of it was that she was just...so angry with him for abandoning them, for not accepting any help. For clearly being *bothered* that someone else had saved him rather than himself doing the saving.

Shay blew out a breath. Maybe she'd figure out how to let that go, maybe she wouldn't. The important thing right now was to focus on the plan. God knew he had one.

"I have the beginnings of a plan," he said, as if he could hear her thoughts. "But I figured you'd want a say in them, so they're nebulous as of yet."

She tried to hide her surprise. Granger was not one for *sharing* plans, or listening to other people's *say*. He was used to being in charge. To barking out orders.

"But first, we need a place to stay. I imagine you have meds to take or bandages to change or something, and then we can plot out how we think we're getting into a supposedly dead mobster's Idaho off-the-grid commune."

"There's one thing I know for sure," she said. "No matter how off the grid this compound is, *Frankie* isn't." A man who wanted to pull strings didn't remove himself from that power source. He simply moved the power source.

"Well, look at that, Shay. We agree on something."

GRANGER PULLED UP to the small rustic cabin in the middle of absolutely nowhere. Though he didn't have a specific plan for how this was going to go from here on out, he'd definitely been making some plans for how to get to this point.

When he'd realized Shay was going to make a move, and alone, he'd made sure his options were in place and ready.

He unlocked the door and let her inside. Shay said nothing as she looked around the place. She hadn't even asked any questions about where the car had come from, where they were going, how he knew to stay here.

She was keeping her questions to herself. He didn't know why that rubbed him the wrong way, so he tried very hard to act unbothered.

"This should give us a day or two to figure out how we want to move forward. It's far enough away from the compound they won't be looking for us here, and isolated enough North Star won't be able to suss out our location either."

Still, she said nothing, just stood in the entry of the cabin, clutching her bag and looking around like she was taking everything in.

When she finally glanced at him, there were no questions. No demands. No excitement to move forward in making plans. There was only hurt in her gaze.

"You knew before I did, didn't you?" Shay asked. There was something like betrayal in her tone and Granger tried to pretend he didn't hear it. *Feel* it.

"Knew what?"

"That Frankie was in Idaho. Alive. Plotting." She let her bag drop to the ground. "You knew for a lot longer than I did."

He had no reason to feel guilt over that. After he'd been shot and nearly died in the explosion that had destroyed North Star's headquarters, he'd begun to question who exactly the Vianni family consisted of these days.

Sure, a mob family could hold a grudge, but most of the ones left had no love lost for Frankie. Anna had told him a small faction of the family wanted to find a way to oust Frankie. So, they should have been glad when everything Granger had been a part of back in Chicago had taken him down.

Not found a way to come after him, even if it was in connection to something else. The only explanation in his mind had been… Frankie. Mobsters had faked their deaths before. Why not him?

"How long have you known he's alive?" she asked with no inflection in her tone.

"Shay, come on. Why does it—"

"How long?" she repeated, but this time there was more heat to it. A little fire in her eyes which eased some of the guilt. If she could be mad, things might be okay.

"I don't know. I've lost track."

"Over a year?"

Granger blew out a breath. "Yeah."

"Two?"

He shook his head. "I started looking into it a few

months after the explosion. I'm not sure how long it took me to find proof."

"Proof," she echoed. "So you had the *thought* he was alive and hiding out even before that?"

Granger flung up his hands, and then realized he was letting her get to him when he'd promised he wouldn't. He wouldn't let weird emotional tangles interfere with what had to be done. How was he losing that battle already? "What do you want me to say?"

She laughed. Bitterly. "I don't know. I don't know what I expected. You have never, ever, not once trusted me."

"Not *trusted* you? You've always been my right hand. I bent rules for you. I let you *question* me. I *gave* you North Star—"

She scoffed, an actual unladylike snort. "You didn't trust me to lead North Star. You couldn't just back off and let me lead. You always had to be there and—"

"You think that's the reason I couldn't let go?" He bit off a curse.

North Star had been his *everything*. After Anna's murder, he had put all that was left of him into a group that would take down the men that had been responsible for that murder. And so many others. It had been revenge, sure, but it had also been about doing something…since he hadn't been able to do something when it had counted.

North Star had been his creation. Where he'd slowly come back to life again. Where he'd first felt like maybe he could survive, and maybe if he did enough good, the loss of his wife wouldn't weigh quite so heavy.

Shay had been there for that, and could still think his inability to let go was about *trust*? "You don't know me at all, Shay." Which was fine. What did it matter? Maybe no one else had been in his life this long, maybe no one else…

It didn't *matter*. "All that matters is making sure Frankie can't hurt you again. So, are we going to get to work figuring out how to do that or do you want me to flay myself open with apologies I don't mean?"

"You knew he was alive and you didn't tell me," she said, and there was no emotion. Just a blank sort of intensity. "Which meant you left me more vulnerable than I needed to be."

"You didn't exactly rush to tell me once you figured it out, did you?"

"Because Frankie punished you already. He made sure you knew he was instrumental in letting the Sons get close enough to Anna to kill her. As far as he's concerned, I'm the one who escaped unscathed. This is about *me*."

"I need a drink," he muttered and moved off to the kitchen. Because if he didn't, he'd say something they'd both regret.

And there were already enough of those.

Chapter Three

Shay didn't follow him at first. She was too…hurt.
She didn't want to be. So he knew Frankie was still
alive before her and hadn't told her? She knew he
would have brought it up if she'd been in immedi-
ate danger.

But this was the problem with Granger. He was
solitary. He did things in his own mind, his own way
and only ever let you in when the deed was already
mostly done.

That had been fine and dandy when he'd been
leading North Star and she'd been a field agent,
working to break down the Sons. She hadn't needed
to know each individual mission's goal. Instead,
she'd followed orders because they were all leading
to the main purpose.

Then he'd expected her to step in and lead. Without any warning, help or guidance. And she'd tried
her damnedest to do her best. Sometimes she failed,
but she had never buckled under the heavy weight
of pressure and guilt.

Granger should have seen that. He should have told her the moment he suspected her *husband* was alive. Shay rubbed at her chest, where it ached with a million emotions she couldn't all parse.

Maybe trust wasn't the right word. Maybe he'd trusted her. She didn't know. But he'd never let her in. Never treated her like an equal.

If they were going to do this—actually beat Frankie once and for all—he was going to have to.

She marched after him to tell him just that. To make it clear. To lay out how this was going to go— in other words, not like it used to. They weren't boss and subordinate any longer. Savior and saved. This might be *about* the past, but it wasn't the past.

But when she entered the kitchen, he was bent over, hands gripping the counter. The bottle of beer sat next to his hand, unopened.

She had seen him angry. She had seen him… devastated, after Anna had died. She'd seen him wrap all that up and pour it into North Star. And then let it all die out when he'd been trying to recover from his gunshot wound and had just… seemingly given up.

He'd shut them out, but he'd always been at the fringes. Like a disapproving parent.

But she had never seen him look…whatever this was. Frustrated? Unsure? Maybe even just the slightest bit guilty—even if he was irritated with himself for being so.

"I did what I thought was right. I've always done

what I thought was right," he said, a slight gravel to his voice that spoke of an emotion Shay didn't know what to do with.

"Must be nice." Because she couldn't be kind when he made her feel soft. She had to fight back.

He shot her a look. "Doing what you think is right isn't always doing right, Shay. Sometimes you learn too late it was all wrong."

That she understood. So well she wanted to cry. But she hadn't cried in front of him since that night he'd gotten her out of Chicago, and she'd promised herself a long time ago she never would again.

When she trusted herself to speak, she kept her voice even and firm. Like she did with subordinates. "There's a lot of baggage here. A lot of past issues clouding the current issue. We need to set it aside for now. The task at hand is to stop Frankie. For good. It's not about keeping me safe, because he wants me to suffer not die. Or at least suffer *before* I die. So this is about protecting the people he might hurt in my name. And it's about putting the past to rest once and for all."

Granger studied her for the longest time. There'd been a time when she'd let herself get a little too invested in the ever-changing colors in his hazel eyes. When she'd been a little too curious about the small scar that marred his lower lip.

She found old habits died hard when it was just the two of them.

"All right," he said, slowly. Then he released his

grip on the counter and stood up straight. "You do whatever you need to do to take care of your wound and I'll get my computer and bring up the map."

She gave a short nod and retraced her steps to her bag. Finding a bathroom, she set about changing her bandages and taking a few aspirin. Afterward, she washed her face to try to wake herself up a little. And then she returned to the kitchen.

Granger had a computer on the kitchen table and was sitting there, frowning at it and writing notes down on a little pad of paper. She stopped short because he was wearing…glasses.

He slid them off his face once he realized she was there and shrugged. "Getting old."

She found her voice, not sure why that had shocked her so much. "Aren't we all?" She moved to the table, keeping a careful distance between them as she peered at the map on his laptop screen.

She slid another look at him. He'd put the glasses back in their case and moved it somewhere she couldn't see it. Like he was embarrassed. Like needing corrective eyewear was a weakness.

She'd once thought him a kind of god. Incapable of getting old or making mistakes. She'd attempted to build herself into the same.

But people were not perfect or godlike. They were continually fallible, no matter how good they tried to be.

Granger had always tried to be good, and clearly in his own mind that meant having no weakness. Or *showing* no weakness. Now that she'd tried to live her life that way she understood how impossible it was.

She blew out a breath and focused on the computer. She didn't need to understand Granger, or feel sorry for him or worst of all, forgive him for the ways he'd abandoned her.

But she had a bad feeling that by the end of this she was going to end up doing all three.

"Vianni's compound is here. We're here. I figure once we have a plan, we fly closer. I've got places I can land here, and here." Granger pointed at the general area on the screen. "I haven't been able to tap into how many men they've got. That's the main challenge we're up against."

He slid her a look, because they both knew who could get them that information, but it brought in people she'd purposefully cut out of this mission.

Granger had found Elsie Rogers himself. Their current head tech, Elsie, was a genius when it came to computers. She was one of his few North Star hires who didn't have any connection to the Sons of the Badlands, and Elsie had proven herself time and time again until she'd vaulted up the ranks in his tech department.

But Elsie was also…a sweet girl, all in all. And she loved Shay like a sister. She wouldn't do what they asked and keep the rest of North Star out of it. Nor would any of her team.

Granger thought about the people he knew outside

of North Star, but the past two years he'd done a hell of a job pulling back from his contacts. Of isolating himself on the old dilapidated ranch he'd bought.

"What about Cody?" Shay asked.

"Wyatt, again?" Granger grumbled. Cody Wyatt had once been one of his better field agents. A sharp mind, a great background—including tech, and a personal need to take down the Sons of the Badlands. But he'd told people about North Star, and once a person did that, they couldn't stay on as an agent.

At least when Granger had been in charge.

Granger figured Cody hadn't wanted to anyway. He'd found out he had a daughter and wanted to build a life. And he'd done it. So, Granger had been done with Cody.

Until Elsie had brought Wyatt into the last mission when Shay had been stupid enough to try and handle everything on her own.

"Cody's almost as good as Elsie with computers," Shay continued. "And he won't alert the entirety of North Star. Especially if I ask Nina to make sure he doesn't."

"I'll never understand how you're friends with his wife." Which was something he should have kept to himself. It was none of his business. Shay's relationships now…or then.

"Why wouldn't I be friends with her?" she replied, squinting at the computer screen.

Granger decided to stop being an idiot and keep

his mouth shut. He should change the subject, but he found his mind was inconveniently blank.

Eventually Shay looked over at him, pale eyebrows raising. "You think Cody and I hooked up?" She laughed, not bitterly exactly. But she was hardly amused. "You are something else, Granger."

"You went on a lot of missions together," he grumbled. He'd *put* them on a lot of missions together. Until it didn't bother him to do so. Because Cody and Shay had always clicked. And that had been fine. Dandy.

"Yeah, it's impossible for a man and woman to work a *mission*, life or death usually, without jumping into bed together?" She raised an eyebrow at him. "Are you really that childish?"

"Don't pretend like there wasn't something between you two. I was there."

Shay shook her head, silky blond hair swaying with the movement. "We were friends. It was never more than that. He was hung up on Nina his whole life."

"Ah."

Her eyes narrowed. "What is that 'ah' supposed to mean?"

Granger shrugged. "He was hung up on someone else."

This time when she laughed it *was* bitter. "You're unbelievable. I was your best damn field agent for years, and you have to boil it down to having the hots for my partner?"

"I'm not boiling anything down, and you were the best damn agent I had. So, I don't know why you're getting pissed off."

She looked at him like he'd grown a second head. "You really just…don't know how to talk to people, do you? You were wrapped up in your revenge for so long, you've just plain old forgotten how to be a person?"

"Why do you think I didn't come back? Why I bought that ranch? Why I was out there by myself for the majority of two damn years? You think I don't understand that I'd lost touch with everything? It was pretty clear."

Well, that shut her up. She frowned and looked back at the computer.

"Look. Contact Wyatt if you want. If you think he can get us the info we need without putting his family in danger."

"He wouldn't."

Granger nodded. "You've got a way to contact him securely?"

"No. Do you?"

He could lie and say he didn't and keep Wyatt out of this, but that didn't get them the information they needed. And it reeked of a personal issue that he most certainly didn't have.

Maybe Shay was telling the truth. Maybe she wasn't. It had nothing to do with *now*, and the fact that it bothered him even a little was a sure sign he needed to get over himself and his need for control.

Because he hadn't been kidding. When he'd been shot and then the building he was in had exploded, he'd thought he was dead. That he'd worked so hard, been consumed by revenge, only to fail in the last moments.

To die, while the Sons and the Vianni family still were out there hurting people.

But it hadn't been Anna's death that had haunted him. It had been Shay telling him he'd started caring more about revenge than about who he was putting in harm's way.

For months as he'd recovered, that had been the thing that tormented him, weighed on him, made him wonder if he even wanted to get back in physical shape or go back to North Star.

If he couldn't trust himself to do the right thing, how did he deserve to go back to the life he'd built?

He handed Shay his phone that couldn't be hacked or tracked. No matter how little he'd believed he'd deserved it, he hadn't been able to stay away from his old life. From figuring out Frankie was alive.

From doing this.

Shay wanted to put the past to rest. Granger felt like maybe he was still trying to make up for his.

If they accomplished this, maybe they could both be free of that. He slid Shay a look as she dialed Wyatt's number.

What would either of them do with that kind of freedom?

He wasn't sure he wanted to know.

When she got off the phone, she turned to study him. Her blue eyes were cool—a clear sign she was still mad about him insinuating she'd had a thing for Wyatt.

"He should have the information we need in a few hours."

Granger nodded. "Then we'll fly out in the morning."

Chapter Four

They ate dinner in near silence, occasionally talking about the area the Vianni compound was located in. Shay mostly didn't speak because she was still irritated about their conversation about Cody.

Still, she couldn't deny that adding Cody to this mission, no matter how tangentially, was complicated. All because, once again, of that mission two years ago.

Granger had used Tucker Wyatt, Cody's brother, to help take down some Vianni and Sons members in the mission that had ended with Granger's nearly fatal gunshot wound. But some of the background had been a lie.

Vianni had been entwined with the Sons of the Badlands for much longer than Granger had let on to the Wyatts. A lie that had protected Granger's and Shay's past from coming to light.

But the past didn't stay buried. Hell, even her husband hadn't stay buried.

They went to separate rooms to sleep, setting separate alarms to get up before dawn and head out to the airfield. Granger made coffee in the morning, but he went and drank his outside while she drank hers in between rebandaging her wound and taking her meds.

Her gunshot wound was healing. She definitely felt stronger, but it was a severe handicap in all she'd want to do if given the chance to come face-to-face with Frankie.

She still vividly remembered the first time he'd hit her. The dress she'd been wearing. The look in his eyes. The shocking, searing pain of a backhand to the face.

Because he was Frankie Vianni. He didn't need to hide the fact he knocked his wife around. It made him look strong to the people who mattered to him.

She'd like to return the favor, now that she knew how to backhand. Now that she knew how to fend for herself. Now that she understood, wholly, the difference between right and wrong. What doing *right* could feel like and accomplish.

She stepped out of the bedroom, her bag slung over her shoulder. Granger was waiting by the front door, looking down at his phone. Brooding.

It didn't matter how long she'd known him now. That she knew just how he'd loved his wife, mourned her probably even now. And rightfully so. Anna Vianni-Macmillan had been a strange blip of good and sweet in that viper pit. Shay had never wondered why Granger had loved her as fiercely as he had.

It didn't matter that all the hero worship she'd had for him in those early years had tarnished in the past two.

He was still too damn attractive for her own good.

Had a thing for Cody? She'd *wished.* Shay had desperately tried to cultivate one so she'd stop pining for a man she knew was so far off limits they didn't even exist in the same universe.

You do now.

She almost laughed out loud at the thought. No, there was far too much baggage between them, even if they were far closer to equals than they'd ever been.

He said nothing when he looked up to see her staring at him. Instead, he just nodded toward the door, and she jerked her head in assent.

They drove, in that same complete silence, back to the airfield they'd used yesterday. The office was empty this early, but that didn't stop Granger. He expertly opened the small hangar, taxied his plane out to the runway.

He threw his bag in the back, then hers.

"Do you think I'm still legally married to him?" Shay mused aloud. Maybe in part because she wanted to remind Granger she was no innocent bystander here. Maybe she'd been young and dumb, but she'd gotten herself into her own mess. He'd saved her once, but he didn't need to save her again.

"Well, Veronica Vianni is legally dead. We made

sure of that. Frankie Vianni is too, so I kind of doubt it." He motioned toward the plane. "Hop in."

She blew out a breath and tried not to pull a face. She wasn't afraid of flying, even in these tiny old planes Granger loved so much. But her gunshot wound made the cramped, jarring ride more than a little uncomfortable.

Still, some things had to be done. She climbed in, trying not to wince or groan as she settled herself into the back seat and Granger into the front. He started the engine in quick, efficient moves.

"You couldn't get a plane that was built in this century?"

He looked over his shoulder at her with a grin—she had not seen him do that in so long, and now it was twice in two days. Had Granger found some level of peace in his solitary ways these past two years?

"Why mess with perfection?" He ran his big scarred hand lovingly over the dashboard and Shay looked away, into the bright blue sky they'd be flying through soon enough.

He began to taxi down the grass field, and the vibrations of the plane went down into her bones. She really didn't understand why Granger enjoyed this so much.

Until they took off. Up above the trees and into the sky. It was hard not to understand the appeal of being above the world, above your problems. Untethered.

They flew for a while, and her mind wandered. She didn't let it go backward into the past. Only forward into how they would approach Frankie's men.

Cody's computer skills had hacked into a security system at the Vianni compound. The place had security access to eight people. There could be more of course—service people who weren't granted that kind of entry, family members who never came and went.

But the main people they needed to worry about were the people of enough importance to get clearance.

The plane shuddering brought her out of her thoughts. She frowned at the back of Granger's head. They usually didn't hit too much turbulence this low.

He was messing with dials. She couldn't see his face to examine his expression.

The plane shuddered again, harder this time, with the addition of the engine making a slightly different sound.

Shay leaned forward around Granger's headrest. "Granger?"

He didn't look back at her. "The plane's been tampered with," he said. "I've lost all my fuel."

Tampered with? Vianni? How did they know... "How. Damn it, Granger. *How?*"

Granger swore, flipping dials and gripping whatever parts of the plane steered the dang thing. He didn't answer her question, and she understood why.

The plane was making terrible grinding noises, and he was doing everything to stop them.

Shay didn't demand anything else. She didn't even watch him work—she knew nothing about planes. Instead, she did something she hadn't done since she was a little girl, and maybe once when she'd pulled Granger's lifeless body out of that burning building two years ago.

She prayed, quietly to herself as things coughed and screeched and jangled. A cacophony of noises that had her stomach twisting in terrible, terrified knots.

But what came next was so much worse.

Silence. Nothing but absolute silence.

THERE WAS NOTHING he could do from here to get the plane restarted. That he knew without even trying. But training demanded that the first step of any kind of failure was to do the most important thing: keep flying the plane. Everything else could come later, but getting the plane into a decent glide without losing too much altitude was imperative.

His guess was the fuel line had been given a slow leak so they could get up and in the air. Get closer to Vianni territory, so that Vianni could deal with the wreckage. If they knew he was the one flying, they knew that he might be able to land the plane without any injuries.

They wouldn't leave it to chance.

Besides, if they really wanted him and Shay dead,

there were far easier ways to murder them. This wasn't about death.

It was about *payback*.

But he couldn't worry about any of that if he didn't land this plane.

The engine had been tampered with too based on the sounds, and he was struggling to turn the plane. Control mechanisms. Whatever they'd done, it was brilliant, because none of it had malfunctioned until they'd been in the air awhile. Some kind of timer, maybe?

Again, something to worry about later. Right now, the mountains were going to make it one hell of a challenge. He needed more room to get the plane into a safe glide, and he needed somewhere safe to land. He needed better control of the plane, and that just wasn't happening.

Whoever had done this to them had timed it perfectly. Because ten or fifteen minutes ago, there were visible fields he could have attempted to set the plane down in. With better controls, he could turn around and glide easily back to those landing spots.

He needed flat land, not the jagged peaks that surrounded them. Still, he worked to keep the plane in a steady glide as he searched the horizon.

He didn't look back at Shay. Didn't think about her. *Couldn't.* His only focus was on landing without inflicting injury on either of them. Not what she was doing or thinking or worrying about back there.

The snow would make any landing difficult—not

just because of possible ice and slick conditions, but because it could hide treacherous rocks and rougher terrain than he could safely land on.

He wished he knew these mountains better. But he'd grown up in the Midwest, spent years in South Dakota. The jagged peaks of the Tetons were still new landscapes to him. He didn't know all their secrets.

He spotted what looked like a flat area that gave him the space to glide into a landing pattern. He studied it as they flew over. From this distance, it looked flat and pristine. It could be snow cover on a lake, but that wouldn't be the worst thing.

The worst thing would be rocks.

He circled it, fighting with the controls to get the plane to turn with no engine to propel him. It took longer than he wanted, and he lost some of his altitude, but he was still in a decent glide. He could still make this work. "Okay, we're going to land here in this patch of flat terrain." *Please let it be flat.* "You're going to want to brace yourself. It might be a little bumpy."

"Shouldn't you radio for help?" Shay asked from behind him, still yelling as if the engine was on, even though there was nothing but the wind up here.

He'd thought about the radio, but in the end, it gave away too much. Especially since the Viannis were clearly already aware of his plane, where they were going, and likely had a plan once he landed.

"The call would go out to the hangar where the

plane was tampered with. Better to keep on the down low and then try to contact someone we trust with my phone when we're on the ground."

"Granger—"

"It's fine," he said, reminding himself not to grip the controls so tightly. "Sit back. Hold on." Then he tuned her out and focused on what had to be done to get them on the ground in one piece. If she spoke, he wouldn't know. His entire being was focused on bringing the plane down smoothly and safely.

It was hard. To keep the glide he needed to be able to move up and down, but he couldn't lose too much altitude too fast or the landing wouldn't be where he wanted it. Everything had to go perfectly.

He managed to turn, though it was a fight with the controls. He managed to slow and narrow in on the field of land.

Everything was going right.

Until it went all wrong.

Chapter Five

The entire plane jerked, and then Shay felt herself flying forward into the seat in front of her. It jarred her wound and she couldn't bite back the cry of pain. But then she was falling to the side, the entire plane…flipping.

Shay reached out and grabbed something—anything—to try to keep herself from getting banged around. She braced herself with her arm as the plane jerked and tumbled. It was rough, but slow enough she could keep herself braced and not suffer anything more than knocking an elbow or knee against the small back seat.

She had her eyes screwed shut, her arms out straight to keep her from falling. She was breathing heavily, but slowly came to the realization that the plane had stopped moving. They were on the ground. In one piece. Well, she was *mostly* in one piece. A little bumped and bruised, but certainly not dead.

Shay opened her eyes and peered out the window.

The plane was on its side, but aside from that wing that had to be broken, it was in one piece too.

"Granger?"

There was no response and a thump of fear went through her as she scrambled to get into a position where she'd be able to see into the cockpit.

He was slumped over the control panel and crumpled into the corner. Ignoring the pain in her side, she climbed over the seat divider into the front. It was too cramped for two people, so she was half on top of him, but she had to make sure…

She swallowed at the horrified lump in her throat. Reaching over, she pulled him up off the dash. His head hung limply to the side and his eyes were closed. His head was bleeding profusely, in rivulets down his face. But his breathing was strong. She could feel the breath puff out of his mouth, feel the rise and fall of his chest.

Shay let out a shaky breath. *Alive.* They were alive. She needed to clean him up, but she'd never be able to do it in this tiny tin can.

She managed to reach over him and kick open the door, but it only flew back shut—a combination of wind and gravity.

Shay swore, searching the plane for an easier way out. The front window was cracked. Maybe she could shatter it completely and they could escape through it—but it seemed like too much work when there was a working door right there.

She'd just have to climb over him to keep the door

open and then…pull him out somehow. It didn't matter how. Just *some*how.

She rearranged him so his head was gently leaning against the seat cushion. Then she awkwardly moved over him until she could push the door open with her hands. She poked the top half of her body out and looked around.

The plane had landed on the snow, seemingly smoothly, but then had hit a big rock. She assumed that's what had caused the plane to flip.

Didn't matter the cause, she realized, *because she smelled fuel*. That was *not* good, particularly since they'd supposedly lost all their fuel. They had to get out of here.

Trying not to panic, she rearranged herself every which way she could think of to pull Granger out of the door. But it just wasn't possible. He was too big and too heavy and her leverage wasn't strong enough. She'd have to get behind him and push him out, maybe.

Shay crawled back in, muttering things to him about what she was doing while she pulled him up and managed to edge her body behind his.

She grunted at the exertion and pain in her side. Granger mumbled something too but still didn't move, so she pushed him again, this time managing to get his body in the right direction.

"The hell you're doing?" he managed to say.

She didn't know if his eyes were open or if he was conscious, so she kept pushing. "Can you get yourself out of the door?"

"I can…" He moved a little on his own, but it was sluggish. "I'm bleeding."

"Yeah, pretty badly too. Let's get out of this plane so we can clean you up. Can you move?"

This time his movements were a little bit stronger and he managed to pull himself toward the door. It took some time and she had to give him a boost, but he finally managed get himself out.

Shay followed, grabbing him at the last second before he fell off the side of the plane into the rocky snow below. She let out a long, colorful swear as pain lanced her side. But she didn't loosen her hold on him.

"I got it," he said, sounding a little more with it. "I can get down okay. Really. Let me go."

"Don't be stupid and try to stand again. You're going to be dizzy. You were out cold."

"No. I wasn't. Just a little fuzzy." He slid off the side onto the ground. He swayed, but managed to stay upright.

Shay pulled herself out of the plane. "Out. Cold," she repeated, looking at how she was going to slide off the side. "Speaking of…it's freezing out here." She looked back into the plane. Was it safe to get their bags?

He reached out and tried to pull her off the plane, but couldn't quite reach. "Don't even think about it. That thing could explode. We have to get out of the way."

"We're sitting ducks without more clothes and our guns."

"Shay."

"How about this? If you can stop me, I won't do it." She slid back into the plane. Her bag had a first aid kit, and his likely did too. Plus guns, layers of clothes, and maybe even some snacks that would get them through.

Shay heard him swearing from outside as she twisted and turned to get to the back. She managed to get the bags out. It was a slow process, but in her mind it had to be done. If the plane blew up with her in it… Well, it was a better way to go than freezing to death when the sun went down.

She tossed the bags into the front, then crawled over after them. She hoped she was imagining the smell of fuel getting more pungent.

Shay could hear Granger yelling at her, and cursing himself as he likely couldn't climb back up the plane. "Better watch out," she called, hurling the first bag out. Then the second.

She followed, though she was still uncertain of her path off the plane. She could slide down, but she needed to control the slide and…

Her thoughts trailed off when she heard an odd high-pitched sound coming from the plane. "What's that?"

Granger's eyes widened, then he grabbed her leg and pulled her into a slide. *"Run!"* he yelled when she hit the ground.

THE EXPLOSION KNOCKED him off his feet and reminded him far too much of two years ago when he'd also been injured and trapped in a burning building that had just exploded.

Except he wasn't in a building. Or the plane, thank God. He was in the open. He only had to get back up and run away from the flames.

Shay.

He managed to get to his hands and knees, but his eyes weren't focusing. He had to blink a few times to see right, and by that time he heard her voice.

"Didn't make that head wound worse, did you?"

He managed to get to his feet. The world seemed to tilt, but Shay was next to him and he realized she was holding him up. *Hell.*

He looked down at her and she was clutching both bags she'd *insisted* on going back into the plane and getting.

"Give me one of those."

"Work on getting your own feet under you first." He realized she was pulling him along a few minutes later. Grunting, he looked back at the wreckage of the plane, then at her.

"Your face is bleeding." Not significantly. Just a few cuts and scratches marring her otherwise smooth skin. Her blond hair had fallen mostly out of its braid and snow was melting in it.

And she laughed. Actually *laughed*. "Honey, whatever is going on with my face isn't half as bad as yours."

They kept walking, her hefting those bags and him barely being able to keep himself upright. It wasn't that he felt so terrible, it was just his center of gravity was off and something kept dripping in his eyes. Snow melt?

"You think this is far enough away?"

Granger looked back at the flaming wreckage of his plane. A little pang went through him. Sure, he had a couple planes, but he loved them all. That one had flown him to Chicago for his father's funeral four years ago.

He'd told no one. Why hadn't he *told* anyone?

"Granger? You hear me?"

"Yeah. Yeah, it's good."

She pushed him—a surprise to him since he was half leaning on her—but he landed on his butt on a flat rock.

"Don't move," she ordered.

Shay dropped the packs onto the ground. The snow was deep but hard. The air was…cold. If he thought about it, *he* was cold. And his head hurt pretty badly too.

Better not to think about it.

She pulled a first aid box out of her pack and opened it, setting it next to him on the rock. Then she frowned at the contents.

"All right," she muttered. She came to stand in front of him, now grimacing at his face instead of the first aid kit. "I can already tell you need stitches."

"It'll keep. You're not stitching me up."

"I'm good enough at it."

"Good enough doesn't fill me with confidence, Shay. Just patch it up. I can let you try to kill me when we're somewhere warmer."

"You were unconscious," she said gravely, not letting him stand to move forward. "Out cold for a few minutes. That's serious."

"I've been through worse."

She sucked in a breath at that. "Fair enough," she muttered. Reaching out, she gingerly touched his hair, slowly and carefully pulling it back from his forehead.

Their eyes met. Held. He couldn't read her expression. Sometimes, he thought he knew her better than anyone else in the world, and sometimes she confused him beyond reason. That searching look was on the baffling side.

He hadn't seen it much lately. It surprised him to realize he'd missed her looking at him like that. But then she focused on his forehead, holding his hair back and wiping the gash with a disinfectant wipe.

In quick, efficient moves, not once moving her eyes back to his, she cleaned the wound and then bandaged it. She wiped the rest of his face down.

"You lost a lot of blood."

"Head wounds. Look worse than they are."

Her frown deepened into a scowl. "Don't try to BS me, Granger." She shook her head. "I don't understand going through all this to kill us."

"I think if they wanted us dead there were other ways to do it."

She collected the wrappers and bloody wipes, containing them in a bag and then putting it into her pack. "This wasn't enough? Tampered planes and explosions?"

"Why not have the bomb go off while we were in the middle of the air? Or even at takeoff if they wanted us dead?" he asked.

"Why have it go off when we've either crash landed or safely landed?"

He didn't answer her. She was smart enough and experienced enough to answer that question herself.

She swore. "They're going to come for me."

"*Us*, Shay. They're going to come for *us*. They waited until we were together. Separate from North Star. Vulnerable, but together."

She looked around them—craggy peaks, spindly pines, a seemingly arctic world. It was still morning, but the daylight had that faded, winter cast to it. And the cold… The cold was going to be a problem.

Of course, not as big of a problem as Vianni surrounding them, and then likely torturing them. For as long as Frankie Vianni wanted to.

"I know you know what we have to do," Granger said, studying Shay as she still looked at the world around them. "Because if Frankie gets us…"

"Yeah, it won't just be death. It'll be a long, painful, torturous death."

"For both of us," he said, making sure she understood there was no *I* in this particular problem. They were in it together.

She nodded, but still didn't turn to face him."For both of us," she agreed.

"So we have to call North Star. We have to."

She stood there, so still, like a statue if her hair hadn't been blowing in the breeze. If her nose wasn't pink at the tip from all this cold.

"Shay."

She finally turned, giving him a small smile with a nod this time. "Yeah. Call in reinforcements."

He didn't know why, but her easy agreement made him uneasy. But clearly she just understood it was the only choice.

Clearly.

Chapter Six

Shay convinced Granger that if they called in North Star they shouldn't move very far. They walked a little to find a place to camp and set up a defensive position if Vianni did get there before nightfall.

He leaned on her, and that caused a ball of dread to settle deep in her chest. She knew he was trying *not* to lean on her and couldn't manage.

That nasty cut on his forehead needed stitches so he could stop losing blood. He insisted his vision was okay, but she had her doubts it was *clear*. Which would make his usual prowess with a gun and aim a detriment rather than an asset. Granger wasn't strong enough to hike for very long. He'd be useless at hand-to-hand combat in his current state. He *needed* North Star.

But she didn't.

Frankie Vianni was after her, because of a mistake she'd made. Sure, she'd been young, but that didn't mean she was about to let North Star—*her family*—put themselves in harm's way because of her.

She did most of the work building up fortifications in the little alcove of rocks they'd found. She wouldn't leave him defenseless, and he'd already called North Star to let them in on what was going on. They'd be here in a few hours tops. Shay just had to time it all right.

Because she had to leave them all behind, that was for sure.

"We need to get some rest. Even if they know exactly where we went down, it's going to take some time to mobilize and get here."

Granger looked at the makeshift alcove they'd made. There wasn't really anywhere to lie down, but there was a rock formation that would work as a kind of couch that they'd covered with some of their extra clothes.

Even though he was steadier than he'd been, he clearly was ready to get off his feet. He sat down first and she settled down next to him, trying to keep her body relaxed so he didn't suspect she was up to something.

They sat hip to hip, the extra clothes that had been in their packs now being used as blankets. Each of them held a gun. She wasn't sure how she was going to get him to fall asleep, and knew it was risky since he likely had a concussion.

But help was on the way, and she needed to make her move.

"I know I've taken a lot of risks in my life, but getting blown up is one of my least favorite things."

She studied him from her peripheral vision. They'd never spoken of the day of the explosion at headquarters. And she'd always wondered…

"What do you remember about the day of the explosion?"

"As little as possible," he replied grimly.

Shay nodded. It had been a bad day in and of itself, figuring out Vianni was there. Realizing the Vianni goons weren't even there for her, but for Duke Knight, who'd been one of the cops to take down Frankie's grandfather back in the day.

Shay had been torn between a fear of the past and a loyalty to everything she'd made herself into. Torn between what she knew was right, and the way Granger had been going full steam ahead into plans that didn't keep innocent people, like Rachel Knight, safe.

So, it was best to let it go. Pretend she'd never asked. Pretend it never happened.

"I was in the interrogation room with Rachel Knight," Granger said, as if he couldn't help but relive it now that she'd brought it up. "She married Tucker Wyatt, didn't she?"

Shay nodded. She'd been at their wedding. Where all the rough and tumble Wyatt men, born to the leader of the Sons of the Badlands, had been enjoying their wives and families, having eradicated that ugly past.

It had felt like so much hope, she'd wanted to get the hell out of there. The only reason she'd stayed through the reception was because Nina had asked her to.

"We were in the interrogation room with the guy who had Vianni ties, but I didn't know it yet and she did. She used Morse code to warn me against the guy we were in the room with. I knew I had to get her out of there. That we had to work together. But he shot me. Then everything exploded. After that… Well… I don't remember anything until a few days later."

Shay knew she should keep her mouth shut, but she had to know for sure. "No one ever told you how you got out?"

"I never asked. I didn't want to know." He looked down at her, because even though they were both sitting and she was tall herself, he still had quite a few inches on her. "You're asking because you know."

Shay shrugged. "Not really important."

There was a long, fraught silence. She could feel his eyes on her so she kept hers looking straight ahead. At the peaks of the craggy mountains. At the snow. The ever falling sun.

"It was you," he said, as if he'd just found out she was some kind of murderer, not the woman who'd saved him from burning alive.

"I was in there looking for Rachel, so it was hardly a rescue mission. Looked for Rachel, saw you, dragged you out."

"You're telling me you saved my life."

"I just happened to be the one who pulled you out, Granger." She frowned at the peaks in front of her.

Why were they talking about this? She had to figure out a way to get him to fall asleep so she could slip away with a decent enough head start. Rehashing ancient history wasn't going to allow that to happen.

She could still feel him watching her, though he said nothing. She shrugged again, shifting in her cold seat and trying to ignore the fact that the side of her body pressed to his was warm enough. "Why's it matter? You probably saved my life a time or two. We're North Star, Granger. We don't keep track." She steeled herself to look at him, to lift her chin and meet that hazel gaze of his without flinching. "That was one of your rules."

She felt some measure of triumph when he was the one that broke his gaze first. He looked down at his hands, eyebrows furrowed as he seemed to try to work through this new information.

"You were pretty pissed at me that day," he said at last, his voice rough.

Shay wanted to stand up and pace. Because she wanted nothing to do with his complicated emotions. Or the way his voice often held all the emotion he wouldn't show anywhere else.

But she held her ground, though she too looked at her hands. "Yeah, I've been pissed at you lots of days. I'd still pull you out of a burning building if I happened upon you bleeding out on the floor. Just like I'd do for any North Star operative."

"Any other," he repeated, in a way that had her heart jittering in her chest.

She didn't look up. Didn't dare address any of the complicated, tangled emotions filling her up. They couldn't matter.

She had to get him to fall asleep, and then she had to get out of here. To face Frankie on her own.

Just like she deserved.

GRANGER BLINKED HIS eyes open with some confusion. He hadn't remembered falling asleep, and he awoke cold and with his head throbbing as though it had been split in two.

Still, it only took him about fifteen seconds from opening his eyes till he realized he'd made a grave tactical error.

She was gone.

He got to his feet—too fast, so his vision wavered. His head felt like it might fall off his shoulders, and his legs weren't so sturdy under him either. He took a deep breath, focused and then allowed himself the moment to swear.

The world around him was pitch-black except for the riot of stars above. A dizzying array that he didn't have time to appreciate. He pawed around the space until he found his pack and felt the cold metal of his flashlight on top of the pack without having to unzip it.

She'd left it out for him. Why that infuriated him he wasn't sure. Except…how could she be this damn stupid?

He flipped on the light and used it to study the

world around their little camp. *His* camp, because she'd left him.

Alone. Defenseless. *Asleep*.

It shocked him down to his bones she'd deserted him this way. And then he realized he must have been out for a significant period of time, because there were carefully constructed booby traps made of sticks and rocks and whatnot that would have alerted him to anyone stumbling upon him.

But more, she thought she was going to stumble upon Vianni before they stumbled upon him.

Purposefully. Alone.

It was infuriating. He wanted to pound something to dust. Yell into the eerie quiet rustling of night around him. But all he could do was stand there. Impotent. Alone.

Stupid, a voice whispered. *Washed up*.

He shook those self-doubts away. Maybe he'd made a mistake, but Shay had made a bigger one, and he wasn't about to let her get herself killed in the process.

When he finally calmed himself, through the heavy breathing, the raging heart, the throbbing pain that seemed to echo in his head like a drum… But no, that was *tapping*.

A signal.

A North Star signal.

He shone his flashlight beam straight up, then right, left, down. A signal, and hopefully enough to give them an idea where he was.

It was a few minutes of squinting into the dark as he turned in slow circles before he saw the little beam of light. He started moving toward it as it moved toward him.

When Granger finally recognized the man approaching him, he didn't feel any kind of relief. Just a weird twist of disappointment as he came face-to-face with Cody Wyatt.

"Wyatt."

"Macmillan."

They studied each other for a long, quiet moment. Granger had recruited Cody out of a CIA internship. Some of his contacts had told him Cody had a sharp mind and a willingness to bend the rules.

Exactly what Granger had needed at the time. He'd even given some thought to grooming Cody to take over North Star. But the more Cody and Shay had worked together, well, the less Granger had felt that interest or pride in the man.

When Cody had been forced to quit North Star, Granger had used it as an excuse. He'd told himself he'd had the feeling all along that Cody couldn't stick it out. That it had nothing to do with *feelings* and everything to do with *instinct* that he'd pulled away from Wyatt.

He'd been an asshole, plain and simple.

"Rest of the team is this way," Cody said at last. "Follow me."

Granger nodded and followed Cody through the uneven, snowy terrain. He bit back a groan at how badly his head hurt, at how cold he was. He tried to keep his breathing even as he followed Wyatt at a speed that felt close to breakneck.

"Getting old on us, Macmillan?" Cody asked, sounding friendly enough.

Granger grunted. "The head wound doesn't help."

Cody looked back at him. "Yeah, you're going to need that looked at. You could have mentioned it."

"I was afraid someone would bring Betty."

Cody laughed. "You should have realized we were bringing a whole lot more than Betty."

They crested a hill and Granger stopped cold. A little camp was set up, fire going, at least ten people surrounded it along with some pack animals.

"What the hell is this?" he muttered.

Elsie Rogers stepped forward as they approached. Their head tech agent, she had no business being here in the harsh winter night. "Elsie, you shouldn't be here."

She waved a hand, which shocked the hell out of him. Elsie had never *waved* him off. He made her nervous. Even when he wasn't the boss, she'd always scurried to do what he asked.

"But I am here," she said firmly. "You have your phone, I'm assuming, since you called. I sent you a roster. I wasn't sure how much experience you had with everyone, so I figured I'd cover my bases."

He pulled out his phone, found the file she'd sent him, and opened it.

Mission Break Free Roster

Cody Wyatt: former field operative, computer and tactical expert

Tucker Wyatt: former field operative, investigation and tracking

Jamison Wyatt: cop, investigation and tracking

Connor Lindstrom: former Navy SEAL, current operative, pilot, S&R expert with dog

Holden Parker: former field operative, explosives expert, with dog

Vera Parker: former spy, computers expert

Nate Averly: former Navy SEAL, weapons expert

Reece Montgomery: former head field operative, good at everything

Gabriel Saunders: current field operative, weapons and explosives expert

Mallory Trevino: current field operative, weapons and hand-to-hand expert

Zeke Daniels: current field operative, tactical plans, knows landscape well

He'd worked with a lot of the people on the list. Even the ones he hadn't, he'd had *some* interaction with over the past few months when he'd been dragged into a few missions as help.

He looked up at Elsie, who had a tablet in her hands. Behind her was every single person she'd put on that "roster." People he'd recruited. Trained. Some people he didn't know at all. But they were all here, because they'd all worked with Shay.

"We can bring in more people if we have to," Elsie was saying. "But these are the people we trust implicitly. We've got Betty in the nearby town, getting a little medical center set up because I doubt we're getting out of this unscathed."

She stood there, so sure of herself, and she'd always been comfortable with computers, but this was something new.

"Are you auditioning for leader, Els?"

She looked up at him, startled for a second, then shook it away. "No. That job is not for me. But this is for Shay, which means we're all going to use our strengths to get her back and safe. For good."

Granger inhaled. She was right. There was only one important mission today, and all emotions and injuries had to be set aside. "All right, let's put together a plan."

Chapter Seven

Shay was exhausted and hungry, but she didn't dare stop. She needed space between her and Granger and North Star, and she needed to find Vianni. She'd been able to orient herself enough to go in the right direction.

She'd had to bet on the fact they'd come from the general direction of where she'd figured out the Vianni compound was, rather than circle around. If they circled around instead, well Granger and North Star would be there to fend them off.

She tried not to think about that possibility. She understood the Viannis and how they worked, and if North Star hadn't interfered last month, she could have handled them then.

You would have wound up dead.

She scowled at the voice in her head that sounded far too much like Granger. Because, maybe she would have. But maybe it would have all been over. She was willing to die for that.

The sun rose, a pearly pink that softened the harsh silver of moonlight on the snow.

God, it was cold. Why had she needed to make this stand in the middle of a nasty Wyoming winter?

She kept walking, wrapping her arms around herself as she trudged forward. Toward Vianni. *Toward Vianni. Toward Vianni.* It became a chant. A count. An impetus.

When she smelled smoke, she stopped and paused and looked around. No sign of it, but there was the hint of fire in the air. Campfire.

She pulled her gun out of its holster and kept even closer watch as she edged forward, following the smell of the smoke as best she could. Eventually the faint sound of voices and movement could be heard and she followed that.

She slowed her pace, creeping behind rocks that were big enough to hide her from whatever she was getting close to. Boulder to boulder, peeking around each and trying to get nearer to the smells and sounds.

Eventually, she found the source of both. A campsite. She kept her head low as she endeavored to figure out how many men were in the camp and if this was the only one.

She positioned herself behind the rock, gun ready. She scanned the area behind her before she set her focus on the camp when she was sure no one else was in the vicinity.

Shay heard voices but didn't see anyone. Still, she

could tell they were coming from the general area, so she kept her eyes on the campfire. Her eyes ready. One man finally appeared, and then another. They each took a seat around the fire.

She watched and waited. They seemed to be making coffee, and when no other men appeared, she decided this was it.

Likely, there were more men close by, but not right here. If she could pick off these guys, she could get the rest of the men's attention on her, and then either fight them off and demand one take her to Frankie…or—

Well, she wouldn't think about the *or*s. She'd focus on her plan and see it through.

She studied the men. They were roughly the same size, so she focused on the one she could get a better shot off on. She adjusted, breathed, counted and then shot.

The first one went down immediately as the other spun around, already pointing his gun in her general direction.

She ducked back behind the rock, counted to five, then lifted her head again. He was charging her area and she aimed, but he returned fire before she could and she had to duck behind the rock again.

She stood and aimed, but he zigzagged at the last moment as he kept running closer. And closer. Rocks were in *her* way now. And trees. She'd lost his progress and she swore, keeping the rock to her back as a kind of protection.

She watched, and listened, keeping her breath even and her heartbeat slow so she could hear the slightest rustle in the world around her.

Then she heard it, with just a second to spare, as he jumped from the rock behind her. She managed to skid out of the way, turn and dodge a punch. She landed one of her own right in the throat. When he leaned forward gasping for air, she tried to knee him, but he moved out of the way so her knee hit his thigh without doing much damage.

She struck again, but he got a hand up to block the blow. This time, when he punched, the blow hit her right above her gunshot wound and it nearly took her down. But no, she wasn't going to get beaten by one of his *men*. She was going to take Frankie down, face-to-face.

He wants that too, she reminded herself. For one of Frankie's men to kill her wouldn't be revenge enough. He could have done that before she knew he was alive.

So, she fought. She ignored the pain and punched and kicked. Even as he managed to get her into a tight hold, she wriggled and *fought*.

"Where's Macmillan?"

She didn't let the question surprise her. The focus was getting out of this. But she filed it away for when she had the wherewithal to deal with the fact they knew *so* dang much.

For now, her only goal was meeting Frankie on her own terms.

"Macmillan is dead. Just like you're about to be." She managed to get her shoulder mobile enough to twist, then she bent, swiveled and used the full force of her weight to rear her head back and bash it into his nose.

He went down like a pile of bricks. Screaming bricks, but bricks nonetheless. Blood poured out of his nose. Shay swung her pack off one shoulder and quickly unzipped the pocket that would offer her an array of restraints.

When she approached him, he tried to fight again, but he was too distracted by his broken nose. She easily got his hands and feet zip-tied. "Hope someone finds you before you freeze to death," she offered.

Shay swung the pack back onto both shoulders and immediately began to move once again. She took a quick look through their camp to make sure there had been just the two of them.

It appeared to be, but even if Vianni thought they'd be injured in the crash, her gut told her this wouldn't be the end of it. It'd get harder, the closer she got. More men. More resistance. This was likely a test.

She looked around. No one had come running, but they would have heard the gunshots and broken-nose guy's screams. They would have sent off some kind of alarm. She needed to keep moving, because intercepting the next round of Vianni men would be necessary to keep them from getting to Granger.

Shay grabbed one of the untouched mugs of coffee, drank it and then scooped some snow to douse the fire.

Then she went back to her long hike.

GRANGER FOUND IN many ways it was easy to slip back into the role of leader. After all, he'd been heading up North Star for more years than he hadn't. He knew how to throw together a tactical plan quickly, how to assess the people looking to him for leadership in the blink of an eye. He was naturally good at this and had the experience to back it up.

But there were things that didn't settle on his shoulders as easily as they once had. The heavy weight of the ticking clock that the more time they sat here and planned, the more danger Shay got herself into. And even though he hated it, he understood, to a small extent, what she was trying to do.

None of these people were inextricably linked to Vianni. They were simply linked to Shay, here for Shay.

And that was the last piece he didn't know how to reconcile with his former self. He wasn't doing this for the greater good. Or even for revenge. Somewhere along the way he'd accepted Anna's death and that need for revenge had slowly dried up into something else. Regret maybe. Some self-blame, sure. But not the fury that had once driven him.

He was here, assembling this team, figuring this out for Shay and Shay alone. No matter how little he wanted to admit that to himself. And that made his nerves coil tighter than ever.

"You're not on either of these teams," Cody said as Granger handed out assignments.

"No. They know I'm out here, Even if she tells them I'm dead, they know I'm out here, and Shay may not believe it, but they want me as much as they want her. I'll follow after her as if I'm on my own."

Wyatt looked at his brothers, exchanging some look that communicated more than words. "I don't think—"

"He's right," Elsie said. She looked at everyone who frowned at her. "Surprise is our best weapon. If they don't know Shay and Granger have backup, why let them know?"

"Because it leaves one of our men defenseless," Cody said, arms crossed over his chest. "*That's* against North Star policy."

"You're not North Star anymore, Wyatt," Granger returned coolly.

"Last time I checked, neither were you."

Granger smiled, or scowled. He wasn't sure. "So we don't have to follow the rules, then." He looked at the people standing around him. They didn't have much more time. Even if Shay found Vianni men and convinced them he was dead, they were going to need confirmation. They would come to the crash site and they would run into this group first.

They needed to get to work.

"I'll follow. Alone. That's nonnegotiable. We

have to use surprise and our numbers against them. They're not stupid. They won't be as clumsy as they were two years ago." Granger looked pointedly at Cody and Tucker, who'd been a part of that disaster.

"Clumsy? Didn't they shoot you and blow you up?" Tucker asked.

"I was a bit clumsy myself," he returned, trying to keep himself emotionally detached. And failing. "Which means both sides have had the time to fix the mistakes they made last time. Holden, you're in charge of the front group, and Reece, you're in charge of the back. Elsie, I want you somewhere safe to run computers."

Elsie nodded. "I'm headed to where Betty set up a clinic once we disperse. I've got cameras on everyone but you."

"We can't risk having one on me. No cameras. No comm units."

Elsie shook her head and opened her mouth to argue, but Granger held up a hand. "I want you all to move out first so you have a chance to surround their compound before Shay or I get there. Any questions?"

There were shakes of the head and then the soft murmuring of chatter as the groups packed up and began to move out. Granger trusted them all to accomplish their tasks. More backup and setup than an all-out assault on Vianni.

He hoped he and Shay could handle that part

themselves. He glanced at Elsie. There was one horse left for her. Granger didn't like it.

Which, he assumed was written all over his face.

"I'll ride down to where we've got a vehicle stashed, then drive to Betty. I'll be fine," she said reassuringly.

"You shouldn't be alone."

"I can handle myself. Promise." She pulled a flashlight out of her pack. "And you can have a comm unit. Looks like a flashlight, even lights up." She clicked it on and then off. "But I'll be able to hear everything going on. And if you push the red button you can talk to me. I won't be able to communicate back so there's no chance they'll overhear anything. But this gives me ears on you."

"Elsie—"

She pressed it into his gloved hand, forced his fingers around it. "You're pretty badly injured, Granger. You're walking into the lion's den. Even if they have a great tech person on staff, they're not going to search your flashlight or care that much about it. Plus, it's got some heft and doubles as a weapon."

Granger took it and shoved it into his pocket. "Satisfied?"

Elsie didn't answer right away. She studied his face as if looking for something specific. "Granger, why do they want Shay? I know you say they want you too, because of this past of yours, but why is Shay so insistent it's her?"

"I think you know the answer to that, Els. Or you wouldn't know what questions to ask."

She frowned a little. "She was married to one of them?"

Granger nodded. It couldn't be a betrayal when he knew Elsie had already found that information out. But he wondered just how much she'd unearthed. "So was I." Elsie's expression didn't register any surprise and Granger sighed. "Those things are supposed to be eradicated from any record."

Elsie shrugged. "If people know where to look, they can find just about anything. And if you recall, you never trusted me with that information, which meant I couldn't wipe it for you."

"I had someone just as skilled wipe it for us."

"Debatable," she replied, her confidence almost making him smile.

But the worry lingered instead. "So, you found out the pasts Shay and I were supposed to have wiped. What can Vianni find on us? All of us?"

Elsie took a deep breath. "Not a lot. I am a genius, after all. But enough, probably, if they know where to start. I've been working on something. I just… don't know if it's the right something."

Granger put his hand on her shoulder. "I'm going to trust you, Els. To figure it out. Okay?"

She nodded. "Okay. Go get her, boss."

Boss. No, that didn't feel right anymore. But he wasn't sure what did.

Except finding Shay.

Chapter Eight

The next group she ran across was larger, but no harder to take down. A campsite of four men, who took turns leaving their weapons behind to go relieve themselves.

Morons.

She picked them off, one by one.

These weren't men from the Vianni compound who would have security clearance, Shay was beginning to realize. These were the kind of paid muscle that Vianni could always find with enough money. Thugs who didn't care what the job was as long as they got paid, or even sometimes men who owed Vianni a favor or two.

Certainly not the kind of men Frankie *actually* surrounded himself with. Eventually, she'd run into the real muscle. The dangerous kind with brains. If Shay had to guess, Frankie was trying to give her a false sense of confidence.

What he forgot, or she hoped he'd forgotten, was that she'd been around when he'd made certain plans.

He hadn't given her credit for being smart enough to pay attention.

But she had. And she knew how he worked, especially now that she had some tactical experience of her own.

Her one worry was that men were spread wider and might move around and get to Granger. She knew she was Frankie's primary target. He wasn't a man who let a wife just run away. He'd likely planned this for *years*.

So, she was the main target and she wanted to keep Granger as far out of it as she could.

Maybe Frankie had some unfinished business with Granger. She couldn't pretend to know all of her ex's twisted vendettas, but he'd been so proud of himself for helping to put Anna in a situation where she'd be murdered. To get back at Granger for some raid or another.

His own sister.

Even Frankie had to consider that revenge enough. In Shay's estimation, he had. God knew she'd regretted all of her choices at that point, enough to see Frankie for who he really was, but she hadn't known how to get out of it.

When he'd told someone about his plans to let Anna die in front of Granger, Shay had realized that somehow she had to get out.

Had to.

And in the way the world worked sometimes, it was Granger Macmillan who'd extended that helping hand. When his men had moved in on Frankie, he'd offered her a way out. When everyone had believed Frankie and his men were dead, Granger hadn't disappeared. He'd offered her the means to serve her penance.

He'd saved her, so even if Frankie was still after Granger, it was Shay's turn to do the saving.

She considered drawing attention to herself. Having all of Frankie's little factions descend on her so they would forget or leave Granger behind. More than once she'd stopped in a clearing, looked around, and considered her options.

Flare? Gunshot? Big bonfire? Or the simple, old-fashioned yell. *Come and get me, Frankie.*

But inevitably she kept walking.

Because, despite everything, she didn't have a death wish. She knew everyone thought these forays into handling this on her own was just that. It wasn't even self-sacrifice as far as Shay was concerned. It was just the way things were.

Frankie was *her* mistake. Now she had to pay for it. Ideally, she'd live through it. And Frankie would be taken care of once and for all.

But if she had to die to take care of Frankie once and for all, then she'd be okay with that. She'd accept that there was a certain poetic justice in it.

She thought of Granger. A tangled, complicated history. They'd never be any more than that.

And if you put this to rest? Survive?

She paused and looked at the dizzying peaks

around her. The snow. The cold. The vast world she hadn't even known had existed when she'd decided to marry Frankie Vianni because it sounded *exciting*.

She'd certainly gotten her "excitement's" worth out of her adult life. So if she managed to survive, maybe she'd seek out something different for once. Something all the people she cared about seemed to be finding. Home. Family. A life.

Shay almost laughed out loud. She wouldn't know the first thing about any of that.

So, maybe it was time. Time to lay the trap. Maybe thirty men surrounded her and she'd be toast, but they'd take her to Frankie first. She would be allowed that final showdown. And she had to believe, no matter how much Frankie had been able to dig up about her life the past ten years, he'd underestimate her skills.

He would underestimate *her*, and she would make him pay.

One way or another.

Shay set her pack in the snow and studied the area around her. But she took her time. She wanted the best chance at survival, and to take out as many Vianni men as she could before they managed to get her.

She worked as the sun shone high above, doing nothing to take the icy bite out of the air. But the sky was blue and the air was clear and the mountains were here. All around her. Strong. Stalwart. Impenetrable.

Frankie might have had a compound in Idaho the past two years, but she bet he didn't understand this place. The land. The sky. He didn't understand the power that came from the world around them because he was a man who thought he'd created the world.

That would be her advantage too.

Shay had her weapons loaded, a good vantage point with rocks as a decent shield from behind. She'd set off the flare and wait and see if anyone moved on her. If not, she'd come up with a new plan.

Before she could pull her flare out of her pack, she heard the faint *thump thump thump* of rocks tumbling down an incline. Someone was coming.

She moved quickly, making almost no noise at all, as she slid between the two jagged boulders that she'd planned as her cover. Then she listened. And waited.

She'd take this new group down and then find some way to attract the rest. If this was another small group of men, and she got them tied up well enough to suit her, she could search their things. Maybe find a comm unit and force one of them to call for backup.

She watched the gun, something strange prickling at the back of her beck. Because this wasn't right. This wasn't the way Vianni worked and…

And she recognized that glove. The stealthy way that shadow moved. "Damn it, Granger."

He stepped out from behind the tree, lowering the gun and smiling at her. Much like he had back at the airfield. Was she ever going to be able to out-smart him?

"Normally I'd offer to let you punch me again, but my head isn't up for it."

THE SHOCK AND anger that went through Shay's expression was at least somewhat satisfying, Granger decided as he watched her try and decide what to do.

He'd surprised her, and that was something.

"I left you behind for a reason," she said, and he could tell there was an attempt at calm in those words. Too bad her delivery was all barely leashed fury. "You should have stayed behind."

He'd promised himself not to lead with anger. From the very beginning, he wasn't going to be the man he'd been toward the end of his North Star days. Angry and bitter and desperate for a revenge that would somehow fix everything.

Now he understood, all the *emotions* stayed. Even when you got exactly what you wanted.

But Shay had always pushed his buttons, no matter what promises he'd made to himself. "You didn't honestly think I'd just let you…run away?" He couldn't think of a better word for it even though he knew that would put her back up.

"Of course not, but I thought North Star would arrive and—"

"Stop me?"

She scowled. "Yes."

"You thought your friends would find me and

stop me from coming to find you? *Help* you?" He
wanted it to come out soft, with just a hint of accu-
sation. A reminder she had an army of people who
cared about her.

But he was afraid that attempt at softness only
sounded like hurt.

She didn't react. Instead, she looked around the
woods, clearly watching for signs of other agents.

He shook his head. "They're not here."

"What do you mean they're not here?"

He could lie. Tell her that he'd convinced them to
disperse. That it was just the two of them. It was a
tempting lie, because it would potentially keep her
safe if she had the stupid idea to go off on her own
again.

It would probably be smart, actually, to keep her
out of the loop. Tactical even.

*Always gotta be the puppet master pulling the
strings.* She'd said that to him once. Years ago. He'd
been surprised by her bitterness, and undeterred by
whatever argument she'd put forth. He couldn't even
remember now, but he recalled the words and the
look on her face.

The expectation he should be better.

"Where are they, Granger?" Shay demanded,
arms crossed over her chest, still standing inside
the little crevice the rocks made.

"I've split everyone into two teams. Their orders
are to stay back, but carefully surround the compound. We'll try to engage with as many of Vianni's

men as possible before we bring them in, so the element of surprise can be used as effectively as possible in order to stop him."

Shay's scowl turned into something softer. Like confusion. "Two teams. How many people are here?"

"Take a look for yourself?" He moved forward, but not close enough for her to be able to reach his outstretched phone. He wanted her out from those rocks, so it felt less like he was the bad guy she was hiding from.

She huffed out a breath and slid out of the crevice and took a few steps toward him. "Someone fixed up your head."

Granger shrugged. "They cleaned me up a bit."

She kept her distance, only stepping as close as she needed to take the phone out of his hand. Then she looked down at the screen, her expression going from vague disapproval to some emotion he couldn't read.

"Mission Break Free," she said. "What is this?" She began to shake her head. "This isn't North Star. This isn't right. Cody and Jamison Wyatt have families. Reece has a family. He retired and promised his wife he wouldn't come back to—"

"As I heard it, Lianna was insistent he come help," Granger interrupted. "If it was to help you."

Shay shook her head. Maybe a little desperately. "No, I don't believe that."

He shrugged. "Doesn't matter if you believe it. He's here. Well, *out there*."

"I don't understand this," she said, her voice tight, and when she handed the phone back to him and quickly turned away he caught the tiniest sight of something that had him stopping cold.

Tears. His heart twisted into a painful knot.

She cleared her throat, keeping her back to him. Then fisted her hands on her hips, clearly working to appear strong and in control. "You have to get into contact with them and send them home."

Even now, she didn't get it. He wondered if she ever would, even if he spelled it out. She was so damn stubborn when she wanted to be. Insular and hardheaded.

Sound familiar?

"Even if I ordered them to go home, they wouldn't. They didn't come because I asked. You keep saying this isn't about me, well here you're finally right. These people came here for *you*. They love you, Shay. That's why they're here. They want to help because you're their family. You mean something to them. I could tell them to go, but they won't. You're going to have to accept that."

She shook her head, the blond braid waving at the motion.

"Why would that upset you?" he asked, wracking his brain for a way to understand this so he could get through to her and they could focus on the task at hand instead of her ridiculous need to handle this alone.

She mumbled something and he didn't catch it.

He moved around to the front of her. "What?"

She lifted her face, and there were tears there. Just a few, dotting her cheeks. "I don't deserve it," she said, enunciating each word like he was dimwitted.

But that didn't make any more sense regardless of how clearly she spoke the words. "Why the hell not? You've fought side by side with all of them." He wrapped his hand around her forearm. "You saved, protected, helped. Why shouldn't they do the same for you?"

She flung her arms into the air, out of his grasp, as she took a few steps back. "You don't get it," she said, too loud for the situation they were in, but maybe they were both a little beyond the situation they were in. "You always fought Vianni. From the beginning, you've been the good guy, Granger. It's like in your DNA." She pointed at him, then thumped her fist to her heart. "I married one of them. I knew he wasn't a good guy, and I married him. On purpose. Because I thought my life was boring and I wanted a little excitement."

She had never really talked about what prompted her to marry Vianni. He'd never asked. Granger supposed he'd assumed she'd been young and vulnerable and taken advantage of. He'd held out a hand to save her that night, because she'd looked terrified. Because she'd had a black eye. Because he knew Anna would have wanted him to.

He knew that victims blamed themselves. He'd seen that firsthand, but he didn't get the feeling Shay was recreating history to make things feel more sur-vivable.

She meant it. Years ago, she'd chosen Vianni. He didn't know what that had to do with the here and now, but she couldn't go on laboring under the assumption they were somehow different.

"I haven't always been the good guy, Shay."

Chapter Nine

Why were they having this conversation? Shay wanted to scrub her hands over her face or maybe dunk her head in snow so she could *focus* instead of get caught up in whatever Granger was trying to do.

He had his own priorities and schemes. This would be another one of them. He knew how to manipulate people. Confuse them. Always for the greater good, but she wasn't interested in being his greater good.

She'd once had the kind of confidence to believe she saw through all that. The past two years had confused some things.

She looked at him, standing in the middle of all this natural beauty, a strong mountain of a man who had always done the right thing, even when he'd lost his way a little bit, trying to tell her he hadn't always been the good guy.

What utter nonsense. She rolled her eyes. "Yeah, you went a little off course a few years ago. That's hardly choosing the wrong side. You let revenge blind you. I didn't say you were perfect. You're human. But you're the good kind. Bone deep. And it's why you loved Anna so much, because she was too. The perfect pair."

"Anna wasn't perfect. I loved her. God, I loved her, but she wasn't some paragon of virtue."

"You forget that I knew her, Granger. You can't lie to me about her."

"No, you forget *why* you knew her. Do you honestly think a woman who spent time with her *mob* family and married a DEA agent didn't have some complicated feelings about right and wrong?"

A knot of dread wiggled around in the pit of her stomach. But that was silly. "Anna was a good person. I know that, Granger. And now really isn't the time to debate your late wife's—"

"How do you think Vianni knew how to avoid some raids, but not others? Why was Frankie always miraculously saved when we'd take down a section of Viannis?"

Shay blinked. She didn't have a good response to that. She'd never really thought about…

"You were married to Frankie. You had to know how many close calls he had. Him and no one else. How do you think that was? They didn't have the dirty cops on their side anymore. It was just them. So how did Frankie slither out from every attempt to arrest him?"

Shay tried to find words, but she was at a loss.

Anna Vianni-Macmillan had been an angel. Sweet to everyone. Good and bright and *loved*.

By both sides.

But no one could be loved by both sides of right and wrong, could they? Not without being a little of both.

"Anna loved her family. She had a soft spot for Gio and Frankie, and they both used it against her. I never understood if she knew she was being used, or if she was naive enough to think they cared about her, but she wasn't immune to their brand of pressure. But she loved me too, so she wouldn't break off the relationship with me *or* her family."

"What are you saying?" Shay demanded.

"I'm saying, Anna slipped them information. Sometimes, if she'd overhear something about a raid or I mentioned where I was going, she'd tell her father." He looked up at her, and there was something there she'd never really seen in his hazel eyes. Not the pain of loss and regret, not that fire of desperate revenge. Just a certain kind of acceptance that the past was what it was. "And I pretended like I didn't know."

She opened her mouth to ask him *why* he'd do that, but she knew. It was all over his face. It had always been all over him.

He'd loved Anna.

Shay could only stare at him. Granger Macmillan had *known* his wife was leaking information to her family—the family he was tasked with bringing down. And he'd loved her anyway. Acted like he didn't know, even though he did.

The noble man so bent on revenge in those years after Anna's murder and he'd...

"Like you said, no one's perfect, Shay. No one's all good, and maybe no one's all bad," he said. "Anna wasn't totally virtuous and upstanding. I certainly haven't been. I tried to be. Good and perfect and always so righteous. God, I tried to be as some kind of penance, but I wasn't. I'm *not*. There's a lot of relief in finally accepting that. None of those people out there helping you think you are perfect. Maybe a little bit superhuman, but not infallible. They just want to be a part of keeping you safe, because it matters to them. You matter to them."

She wouldn't let emotions win again. It was stupid and a weakness she couldn't afford. She'd blame those stray tears on exhaustion and hunger and move right on pretending Granger had never seen them. "Why is it so hard for everyone to understand that they matter to me so I don't want them in the middle of a mess I created myself?"

Granger seemed to take the time to really think that over, and a glimmer of hope went through her. He'd see it her way. He'd understand.

Then his jaw firmed, and he stood there so *sure* about everything. "Because it's insulting, Shay."

"It isn't—"

He grabbed her arm again, harder this time so she would have had to fight him off to escape.

Something she could have done. Easily. But didn't.

"You matter to me, Shay. To not use my skills, my abilities to help you *is* insulting. To not use all that you have at your disposal to help you—not just survive but to take down someone who deserves taking down, the whole damn point of North Star by the way, it's like spitting on everyone who cares about you."

Everyone, but it was his *you matter to me* that struck the hardest. Even now. "Granger..." She wished she had the words to end this. To *stop* this. He couldn't bulldoze her. Not now when it was so important. When half those people out there had families and loved ones and Frankie would kill them without a second thought.

And you too, Granger. Even with all those skills he was talking about. The men Frankie had would have a similar set of skills. They were dangerous, smart and certainly more ruthless than this first wave of men she had already beaten easily.

But wasn't North Star better? Wasn't that the *point*?

"We are by your side," he gritted out. "Now are you going to keep fighting that? Or do we get this done together?"

VERONICA SHAY HAD been in Granger's orbit for over a decade now. First as Frankie Vianni's wife, and thus both his wife's sister-in-law and someone he'd kept an eye on while being part of the agency that had been tasked with taking the elder Vianni down.

Then he'd known her as the young woman he'd saved during the raid that had allegedly killed her husband. Because she'd looked scared and defenseless.

She hadn't been, defenseless anyway. And Anna had been dead and he'd needed men. So, he'd trained her, and maybe she'd been focused enough not to see that he'd groomed her to take over North Star if he ever lost command.

He'd known her through all these transitions, assured himself he understood her, but he hadn't understood the depths of *this*. Some kind of martyr complex mixed with…not survivor's guilt. It was something more like victim blaming, with herself as the victim. Not that she'd ever call herself a victim. She thought she'd chosen the wrong path, and there was no making up for it.

Maybe she'd chosen to marry Frankie, but he doubted an eighteen-year-old girl from a fairly normal family by all accounts had known what she was getting into. There was no way she'd chosen a man she'd thought would abuse her, use her as a pawn and then track her down for some kind of revenge even though he was supposed to be dead.

"I feel *old*, Granger," she said after the silence had stretched on too long. "Old and tired." Which didn't answer his original question, but he knew the feeling.

"Join the club, and consider that I've got another ten years on you."

She slid a look at him, as if studying him for the evidence of that ten years. It was there. He saw it every time he looked in the mirror. What he'd built was a young man's game, and it wasn't so much that he *couldn't* keep fighting, it was more that he'd lost the driving fire within him to do so.

Granger wanted to rest. He wanted to enjoy the ranch he'd settled himself on. Bring it back to life, rather than spend his days worrying about Vianni.

"You want to put the past to rest. So do I," he said, holding that gaze.

She nodded, so faintly he almost didn't see it.

"We started this together, Shay. When you took my hand outside the Vianni house. Let's end it together. Once and for all."

Again, she gave another small, imperceptible nod. "Do you think we can take care of things and keep North Star on the periphery? I couldn't live with myself if any of them were hurt in this."

"We can try."

She nodded, a little firmer this time. "Okay." She swallowed, clearly trying to recalibrate to a new plan. To having backup.

"We'll just do it together," she muttered, looking around the area they were in. "I've got everything set up to fight off as many as I can, but the end result is to be taken to Frankie. I'm not looking to *win*, just to put the odds better in my favor."

Granger nodded. "So a flare?"

"Yeah, and then sit back in this crevice, pick off as many as I can until they surround me. Then surrender."

"Will we both fit in there?"

"Barely, but it's doable."

"All right. Let's do it then. Before dark preferably." He glanced at the sky. The sun was already beginning its descent, but it was worth a try.

When he looked back at her she was frowning at him. "Aren't you going to pick it apart? Tell me all the holes? Take charge and do it *your* way."

"I have learned a lesson or two."

She arched a brow. "You hadn't when I asked for your help on Holden's case."

"You asked for my help on Holden's case less because you needed it and more because you were worried about me."

She looked startled for a moment, but he could tell from the expression in her eyes that he'd hit the nail on the head.

Something turned over in his stomach. An old feeling he barely recognized because his life was so different now.

Nerves. A distinct discomfort with not knowing what to do. When he'd had any indecision trained out of him long ago.

He thought of the raid on the little farmhouse in Nebraska for Holden's last mission. Shay had been shot. Not like last month, just a nick in the arm. It had affected him, in a way he knew meant he didn't have the objectivity he'd once had.

"It's a solid plan, and I don't have a better one," he said firmly. "I'm used to being the leader, yeah. It's a hard habit to break, but I always trained you to be my number two, Shay. I can train myself to treat you like a partner."

She seemed a little dubious, but she didn't argue anymore. A moment later, she got out the flare and set it in the middle of the clearing. "They might know it's a trap, but I figure if that's the case they'll just send more men," she said, pointing the flare gun in the air.

"Which works in our favor."

She nodded, then set it off. The *bang* wasn't exceptionally loud, but the bright light that emanated from it should be seen by anyone within a twenty-five-mile radius. Luckily the mountains they were in were isolated enough Vianni's men should be the only ones.

"North Star won't come running, will they?"

Granger patted the flashlight attached to his vest. "Elsie's listening right here."

Shay inhaled. Apparently she still wasn't *okay* with North Star being a part of this, but she was trying. Eventually she nodded, then pointed to the crevice. "I'll go in first, then we'll see if we can fit you too. Then we wait."

She slid into the crevice and he followed. Granger knew they had to find a way to both fit in the small space, but also still have at least the dexterity to shoot someone if they appeared. They had to move around to get situated, bodies brushing up against each other, her hair sliding across his cheek, the stubble of his beard scraping against the tip of her nose. Once they were finally settled, they were face-to-face. They each had a back to the cold rock encasing them. Luckily, he was left-handed, so it worked that they both had their shooting hands free.

But that was where the luck ended, because the crevice was small and their backs pressed to the rock meant their fronts were pressed rather closely to each other. He could feel the rise and fall of her breath. See the patterns of different shades of blue in her eyes. He could feel every twitch, fidget and tensing of her body.

Which meant she'd feel his and *that* could spell bad news soon enough.

He should look away from her. Stare at the sky. At the world around them. Dimly, he was aware of all he *should* do, but all he could seem to do was stare at all that mesmerizing blue.

Her gaze held his and his heart thundered in his chest.

He should suggest he find another vantage point, another damn crevice. Because this was just the kind of thing he avoided, close quarters. Which meant he should look away, at least, because that was the point of this. Sit here and wait and *watch*. Not her. The world around them.

Her gaze dipped, to his mouth. He expected her to immediately look away, turn her head so they weren't even facing the same direction. They'd been here before, once or twice, a tense moment one of them immediately broke.

But she didn't.

And neither did he.

Chapter Ten

There were a million voices in Shay's head telling her to stop this. *Look away! Don't lean forward! Get out of here!*

There was a tenseness in his body that in any other circumstance she might have read as a reluctance. A refusal. She might have *convinced* herself of that, in any other circumstance.

But that was not what she saw in his hazel eyes, and instead of purposefully getting out of his orbit, she was stuck in this small space, staring right into his eyes. Where a softer version of something familiar she'd seen there before lurked. A version of that *thing* she'd avoided at all costs before.

But it had never looked or felt quite like this.

She knew people could change because of the great, vast changes she'd been through, but she'd never expected Granger to change. At least, not in this healing kind of way. Not when he'd been so bent on revenge. So consumed by grief. She hadn't expected him to become more…*human*. Like some regular guy who might have a life outside of North Star that wasn't the little hermitage he'd built for himself.

But it seemed like maybe he was ahead of her on that score.

She didn't know what to do with that knowledge and still she didn't look away, no matter how much she told herself she should. For ten years she'd avoided *this*. For a wide variety of reasons. She tried to remind herself of *any of them* as his body heat seeped into her. Cocooning her in warmth. *His* warmth.

She was so tired of fighting, wasn't she? And what was this but another fight? Why *not* be done with it? What did it *matter*? If she finally did the thing her body wanted so desperately to do.

So, she put her lips on his. An old daydream that had always embarrassed her, but never gone fully away. Because he was *Granger*, and despite his mistakes he was her paragon of everything she wanted in a man.

The feeling that jolted at the touch of his mouth to hers was so unexpected, so…*big*…she would have bolted away if she'd had room, but she had none. She was stuck here, and maybe she could have turned her head and mouth away, but his hand came up and held her cheek.

Keeping her in place, kissing her back in a far more *adult* way than she'd ever envisioned.

Her stomach seemed to jump on a roller coaster and take off, and she forgot about the cold stone at her back, the men who should be coming for them. She forgot everything. Because no matter that she'd occasionally let herself imagine what it might be like to kiss Granger Macmillan, she had never known how to imagine…*this*.

Because it wasn't superficial or casual like any other relationship she'd had in her life. This was a simple kiss, but it dug deeper than anything she'd ever experienced before. Burrowing beneath her defenses, ones she'd spent a decade building and perfecting.

He pulled away, and it took her precious seconds to realize her eyes had fallen shut and she needed to open them. When she did, she was met with all that hazel, and a small smile on his face she couldn't decipher.

Maybe didn't want to.

What on *earth* had she done? Years of self-restraint and common sense and she'd kissed him in the middle of all this? She really was losing her edge. "That…must have been my head wound."

His mouth curled, just a little at the corner, in a way that had her stomach swooping all over again.

"I think I'm the one with the head wound," he said, his voice low and rough.

She was so dizzy she thought for sure it must be her, but she couldn't analyze any of this. "Granger…"

"We'll put the past to rest. We both need that, but it doesn't have to be the whole past. There were good parts in there, and for me, they were mostly with you."

She was speechless. Utterly.

"But for now, we've got company." He pointed outside. She didn't see anyone, but when she forced herself to *focus*, she could hear the faint sounds of men on the move.

"Els, we're going to take out as many as we can, but the plan is to let them take us. Keep everyone back until we give the signal."

Shay stared at the flashlight he was talking into. He'd said… Oh God, he'd *told* her that Elsie was listening. And she'd…she'd…

"She can't communicate with me, she can only see and hear," Granger reminded her.

But…

"So, she heard and…saw all that before?"

His eyes stayed on the men carefully moving in as his mouth quirked again at one side. Amusement. "Imagine so."

Shay closed her eyes and felt an odd heat climbing up her cheeks. When was the last time she'd *blushed*? And over something so…

"Worry about living through the embarrassment once we've lived through this, huh?" He moved a little, edging toward the front of the crevice. "I'm going to go put up a fight. A dumb one. I'll take one or two down first, but once they've got me and insist you come out, do it. Don't lay it on too thick. Pretend like you don't care about me. Give them what they expect."

Give them what they expect. That was basically the gist of her plan, though she hadn't thought of it in precisely those words. They were on the same page.

Not leader to subordinate. He wasn't saving her.

They were in this…together. Fully. Maybe she'd been afraid that was impossible, when he'd always been the person she looked up to, but now she understood this all for what it was.

Working together. The team he'd made. Because it mattered. Not just ending Vianni, but her herself mattered. To him.

"Granger."

He looked back at her. She would have said he was all business, but there was something about the way his eyes tracked over her face, like he was soaking it all in.

She wished she could give him any of the words he'd given her. Something that would mean… anything. But all she could think to say was utterly stupid. "Don't die."

But he grinned at her. "Same goes, Veronica."

When she scowled at the use of her first name, he chuckled, and stepped out into the fray.

HE KEPT LOW and quiet, even as the men crested the hill.

A hell of a lot of men.

Well, Shay's plan had worked. He'd worried they'd wait them out. Or just send a small, ineffectual group like the ones before. But these guys were bigger, decked out in tactical gear. It seemed each wave was just a little better.

But the question he had was whether this was the last of them. Or did they have bigger men with bigger weapons waiting for them? He wanted to get through as many waves as possible before they surrendered.

No doubt there'd be another set at the compound once they allowed themselves to be taken, so the more they could take out here the better.

Granger ignored the twist of disquiet in his gut. It was dangerous business, letting themselves get captured by a group of well-trained henchmen who wanted to hurt them—not just kill them, but *hurt* them. A lot could go wrong.

But a lot could go right. Even as he braced himself for the first blow from a big man who's guns were still strapped to his side, his mouth curved. So far, things had been going all right, the destruction of his plane aside.

Shay had kissed him.

He might have laughed at the wonder of it, but instead he dodged a meaty fist and dealt an elbow to the gut. Kick, twist, uppercut. He wanted to fight as many of them as possible before he introduced his gun, because even with vests on, and the belief Frankie didn't want them dead before he could torture them a little bit, he and Shay could catch a stray bullet in the fray.

Best to keep the guns holstered for as long as they could.

A man grabbed him from behind and the guy he'd been effectively fighting landed a gut punch that hurt like the devil, but Granger twisted, kicked and had the man who'd attacked from behind howling in pain.

He fought off a few as the rest of the men searched the clearing, presumably for Shay. None of them found her hiding place or even seemed to consider that crevices could hide people.

Still not the cream of the crop, then.

"Where is she?"

Granger shrugged, and used the movement to feign a kick. When the man moved to block it, Granger swung his elbow into his opponent's nose.

Blood spurted along with a scream of pain.

Granger still refused to use his gun, which meant that as many men as he fought off, he was still getting a bit of a beating himself. Enough that he started to slow. One man grabbed his arm and before he could get a punch off, another grabbed his other, wrenching it behind his back. He still had his legs under him and he might have fought them off, but his vision was getting a little blurry. Granger blinked the moisture away, wondering if it was a new injury or his old one bleeding into his eyes. Either way, it severely limited his ability to make tactical choices.

"Where is she?"

"You guys are bad at your jobs," Granger replied. Which earned him another hard punch in the stomach from the man in front of him. He bent over, but the other men still held him as he struggled to breathe from the nasty blow.

"All right, that's enough," Shay's voice said.

Granger would have laughed at the shocked looks on the conscious men's faces if he'd had the breath. They looked around, still clueless as to the location of her voice.

Shay stepped out of the crevice, looking like the warrior that she was. Her blond hair shone gold in the riotous sunset, and her chin jutted out in stubborn disdain.

She didn't point her gun at the sky, or keep it holstered. Instead, she aimed it at the man pointing a gun at her. He was the only one who had his gun out, further giving credence to Granger's belief they wouldn't kill anybody.

Yet.

"Put it down," the gunman yelled, and though most of the other men appeared to be completely calm, this guy seemed a little nervous.

Not a good combo.

Shay took a step forward and the guy's gun went off. Granger jerked against the men who held him, but they were strong and firm and Shay didn't go down, though her whole body jolted.

She glanced down at her vest, where Granger could only assume the bullet had hit. "You're going to regret that," Shay said, looking at the man who'd shot at her.

Granger knew that it must have hurt. Her tactical gear might have stopped the bullet, but the impact was still a hell of a blow. But she acted like it hadn't hurt at all as she charged the shooter.

"Guns down," someone shouted. "Guns down! Those aren't the orders."

Granger used the bolt of panic to his advantage. He wrenched one arm free, used his body weight to pull the other man to the ground and began to wrestle him into submission. He didn't expect to win, more wanted another distraction and everyone to report to Frankie that they had fought with everything they had rather than give Frankie any reason to believe they'd been captured on purpose.

So maybe it was time to pull out his gun and do some real damage. He reached for it, but because his peripheral vision was compromised, one of the assailants caught his arm before he could wrap his fingers around the handle of the gun.

He heard another gun go off, but two men were holding him down now and he couldn't see well enough to figure out if it was Shay or the nervous gunman. He kicked out, managed to dislodge one of the men holding on to him. This time he did get a hand on his gun and managed to shoot the man trying to get back up.

He whirled on the other man who'd held him, but was met with the barrel of a gun pretty much right between the eyes.

"There weren't any orders about you," the man said, his mouth curving into a dead-eyed smile.

Those words sent a cold bolt of fear through Granger, but he wasn't about to go down without a fight. He moved into a quick crouch, but before he could sweep out a leg to take the man's feet from under him, another gunshot went off and the man in front of him went down like a sack of bricks.

He looked behind him to see Shay holding the gun. She'd taken out all the men around her. He looked down at the man who'd almost put a bullet through him, then back at her. "Thanks."

"Don't mention it," she said with a smile, but it faded. "You're bleeding again."

"So are you," he said, pointing to a gash on her arm. She looked down at it as if surprised to find it there, then shrugged.

Without having to say anything, they moved back-to-back as another wave of men moved forward. These guys had even higher-powered weapons, more tactical gear and a size and bulk the previous men didn't.

"I think it might be time to surrender," Granger whispered, eyeing the men and then returning his gaze to Shay. If Frankie had this many men at his disposal wherever they took them, the odds might not be as heavily in their favor as he'd hoped. But he counted, and there were only five of these guys.

If the eight with security clearance was true, that left only a few back at the compound with Frankie.

She looked over her shoulder at him then offered a grin, reminding him of those early days in North Star, when she'd relished the fight. When she hadn't been afraid of anything or felt responsible for anyone. "I hope you're ready for this."

He'd put her in charge and she'd lost that bravado. Because the weight of leadership didn't sit so comfortably on good people, people who cared deeply. Sending people into danger weighed different when you were *invested*.

When they got to the other end of this, he would find a way to remove that weight he'd inadvertently put on her shoulders for the past two years.

He nodded and then slowly lifted his weapon as she lifted hers—in surrender this time.

Together.

Chapter Eleven

Shay stood, still back-to-back with Granger, breathing heavily and trying not to catalogue all the aches and pains she now had after that fight.

It had been a *good* fight. Men so often underestimated her ability to fight—either they treated her like a man because she was tall and built, or they thought they could outmuscle her simply because she was a woman. But she had a grace and flexibility difficult for most men who'd spent time building muscle and strength, and also that strength that so many guys didn't think to acknowledge.

It had felt like old times almost. To let loose like that. To fight simply to fight. With Granger. In the field. Not in charge of anyone or responsible for what happened to them.

Just a fight.

There was a freedom in that, but it was short-lived because she knew that her team, the people who'd become her friends and then her family, were out there, ready to swoop in and save her and Granger. He was mixed up in this because of her, and the fact that the man had been willing to shoot him proved in Shay's mind that Vianni wasn't here for him.

All they wanted was her.

But as they held up their weapons, and this new group of attackers moved forward, Shay had to fight back the fear they'd simply take Granger over to the side and shoot him. If the other man had been willing to—

She was grabbed roughly, and she fought it off instinctually. But the men took her gun and there were three on her, wrenching her arms behind her back and cuffing her. She still wriggled and refused to make it easy on them.

It wasn't just acting so Frankie believed they'd been caught against their will. She had too much pride to subject herself to this *easily*.

Shay managed to crane her neck to see Granger. They were doing the same to him. So no plans to kill him. Yet.

"Take one last look," one of the men holding her said, and then something was being pulled over her head, plunging her into even more darkness than the world around them.

"Isn't this a bit overkill?" she asked, though no one answered. They were out in the middle of nowhere, and night was falling, so what did blindfolding her do?

What did it *hide*?

That question roused an iciness that had nothing to do with the cold settling in her chest. But she wasn't alone. She had Granger, and an entire team of people out there watching and listening.

All ready to move. To act.

She couldn't let fear guide her. Not anymore. She'd been struggling with that for two years now. And while she still wasn't sure she was *comfortable* with all this help when she'd brought this problem on herself by marrying Frankie in the first place, she knew she had to find a way to come to terms with it once and for all.

She was pushed forward, and fought to stay sure-footed in the slippery snow and rocky terrain. Vianni's men wouldn't care if she fell and hurt herself. They would relish it, she had a feeling.

They couldn't kill her, but she doubted she had to be in pristine condition when they brought her to Frankie.

She tried not to think about what he would do, because there were too many terrible outcomes. Number one, killing Granger in front of her if her ex thought she had any emotional attachment to Granger.

And if Frankie knew what she'd been doing for the past decade, he also knew she had *some* kind of connection to Granger.

She swallowed down the wave of fear and horror that she might be walking Granger straight to his death.

But no. No, if that man back there had license to

kill him, Granger didn't matter to Frankie. Even as a means of revenge.

Shay held on to that as she was pushed and pulled forward, trying desperately not to stumble as she walked blindly, too fast, in an uneven landscape.

They wanted her to fall, she could feel it.

Give them what they expect.

She frowned at Granger's voice in her head, but he was right. They'd expected her to fight, so she'd fought. And they'd expected to win, so in the end, they'd let Vianni's men win. Now, they wanted her to fall, and giving them what they wanted was going to help her in the long run.

Besides, planning her fall was going to be a little better than it happening accidentally. So, she slowed her pace until the guy behind her gave her a shove. Then she purposefully fell forward, and a little to the side—both in an attempt to brace herself for the fall and to keep her injured side from hurting more.

Of course, the rocky ground made even the attempt at a purposeful, graceful fall extraordinarily painful. Her shoulder hit a sharp rock, her hip and elbow knocking against hard rocks as well.

She didn't have to feign the cursing as pain shot through her. Her only saving grace was she had managed to land on her less injured side.

"Get up," one of the men ordered, pretending to be inconvenienced, but she could hear the laughter around her. They were all quite happy with themselves for "making" her fall.

She would *enjoy* taking them down. She allowed herself to imagine that as she struggled to get back to her feet. Her side ached where she was hurt, but to make sure they didn't see *that*, she adopted a fake limp so they'd think she hurt her leg on the opposite side.

The men snickered, even more pleased with themselves for having inflicted some harm.

She'd tried to keep track of how long they walked, but it was so dark in the hood, there was no good way. Shay didn't let herself fall again, no matter how much they pushed and laughed, because she couldn't risk severely injuring herself when she was already weakened from last month's injury.

They didn't seem to know about that. Surely Frankie did. He was the one who'd sent the men to hurt her in the first place. And he hadn't given his men that piece of information that might help them make her miserable and in more pain.

She didn't know what to think of that, and didn't have time to figure it out as she was being roughly shoved into something...the back seat of a vehicle.

There was faint rumbling from the men who had to heft her a little bit to get her up into the seat, but no clear indication of what was going on.

She held her breath, anxiety filling her as she wondered if she'd be separated from Granger. What would they do then?

Someone bumped into her shoulder, and she immediately knew it was Granger. Similarly tied up and shoved into the back of a car.

It was a small, fleeting relief, but relief all the same.

"West," Granger muttered, likely to Elsie listening in from wherever she was. Would North Star be able to track the vehicle if they didn't have one of their own?

It didn't matter. They all knew where they were going. Out of Wyoming and into Idaho.

Straight to Frankie's compound.

GRANGER KEPT HIS shoulder pressed to Shay's, just a simple reminder or reassurance they were in this together. It centered him in a way he couldn't identify, and didn't have time to.

He had to concentrate. North Star was far enough out that muttering the direction they were going in so Elsie could verify they were being taken to Frankie's compound would be necessary. They wouldn't be able to follow without getting too close or they'd be marked.

Granger was pretty certain Shay would be dropped off at Frankie's compound. He wasn't so sure about himself. The man back there during the fight had been willing to kill him.

They hadn't done it, but they could have. Easily, when he and Shay surrendered.

Granger didn't know what to make of it. He just

knew he had to keep his mind open to all the possibilities.

And one of the major possibilities he saw was that he and Shay would not be taken *to* the compound they knew about, even if they were taken *to* Frankie. At least at first. At least while he waited to see what North Star would do.

Because as much as this was about Shay, Granger couldn't get over the fact that when she had been shot, there had been an effort to make the people of North Star pay and suffer. Frankie wouldn't honestly think Shay had handled this alone, even if she'd tried to.

Granger hadn't verbalized that to her, in part because he just wasn't certain. It was just a possibility. And also in part because that was exactly what she was worried about and he didn't want to add credence to her worry that the people she cared about might be hurt in all this.

Was he lumped in with all that? Or was he separate? Did that kiss mean…

There was no room for error, for worrying about a *kiss* for God's sake. This was about life and death. Not their *feelings*.

He grunted irritably. At himself…and the situation as every jolt and bump of the car caused another ache in his bruised body.

"South," he muttered. He wished he could hear Elsie talk back. It would be a risk, but at least he'd be able to know what information she had.

He could even be wrong about those directions, about what he felt. It had been a long time since he'd been in this kind of high-pressure tactical situation.

Shay said nothing. She sat next to him silent, keeping her shoulder pressed to his.

Granger felt the car gently turn again, then muttered a new direction toward the flashlight. There were doubts, but at the moment he only had himself to depend on.

The vehicle began to slow and Granger tried not to let the dread creep in. He needed to be alert and ready for whatever was thrown at them.

"Coming to a stop soon," he murmured to Elsie.

"I was just thinking," Shay said, her voice low as the car completely stopped and the men got out. It would only be a matter of seconds before the back doors were opened and they were no longer alone. "Frankie has to know we know where the compound is. Which means…"

"We're not at the compound."

The back doors opened and they were pulled out. There was no opportunity to say anything more or exchange theories about where they *were* if not Frankie's compound.

They were moved roughly for a while still outside, but then Granger heard the distinct squeak of a door and he would have almost tripped over a step if not for the hard, unrelenting hand that grabbed his arm and pulled him up rather than let him fall.

"You're all heart," he said to whoever had him.

There was a grunt but no other response as he was shoved forward—this time without anyone grabbing him or pushing him. He was standing still, and he heard feet shuffle around him—including the hard thumps of what he assumed was Shay being shoved and managing to stumble but balance enough to keep herself upright.

After a moment or two, his hood was pulled off. Even if Shay hadn't come to the conclusion beforehand, he would have immediately known they weren't at the compound Shay had found and been searching for.

The space was too small. Not heavily guarded. This wasn't the kind of space Frankie would spend any time in. It was dirty and rustic, and not meant to bring anyone any kind of comfort.

But this was where they'd been brought. This was where their hoods had been taken off. He didn't dare look at Shay as he studied the room around them. He had to focus on facts, not feelings.

At best this was some kind of holding cell, and at worst… Well, there were a lot of *at worsts* depending on where North Star was.

And what Frankie was planning to do.

ELSIE ROGERS STARED at the map. She'd been able to follow the directions Granger had given her through the mic, but they didn't make sense.

Either he was wrong, or her map was. She had a

bad feeling it was the map, and that it was very purposeful. Someone working against her.

She swallowed at the fear of that. How could she
be working off a false map? And how could someone have the kind of access necessary to make that
happen?

But now wasn't the time for the who or how, it was
the time for how did she fight against what someone
was trying to do to stop her.

She looked back at the information Granger had
given her. She'd written down every direction, and
she knew where they'd started. Maybe her map was
wrong, but she still had the right directions.

"They didn't go where we thought they'd go."

Elsie blinked at the speaker and then scrubbed
at her eyes. She had to *think*. "No, they didn't," she
said to Cody.

"That means we're in the wrong position. We need
to move."

"Yeah."

"Elsie, where are they?" he asked.

Panic threatened to spurt up inside of her, but
she knew that Shay wouldn't panic. Bad things happened, unexpected obstacles cropped up. A person
had to stay calm and in control, no matter how worried they were about the people who might be in the
crossfire.

"I don't know where they are. My computer's been
tampered with." She had to fight back the wave of
fear and failure. Both wanted to win. She was a com-

puter genius and now she couldn't trust her computers.

But as long as Granger and Shay were alive she had the chance to bring them back home. She just had to figure out how to use do it.

She turned off her mic to Cody. "Betty?"

Betty Wagner, resident North Star doctor for the time being, poked her head into the room Elsie had commandeered for her computers. Useless computers at this point.

"We need a map of the area. *Not* your phone or a computer. A paper map."

Betty frowned. "The gas station might have one, I guess." She studied Elsie and then nodded. "I'll go get one."

"You have to be careful."

Betty nodded. "I've learned a thing or two about stealth. Stay here. Listen to the team. I'll be back as soon as I can."

It was Elsie's turn to nod. Once Betty left she allowed herself one shaky breath and then swallowed. She straightened her shoulders and put her mic to Cody back on. "Okay, listen closely. This is what we're going to do…"

Chapter Twelve

Shay knew better than to be thrown by a change of plans. When you were an operative, you had to roll with any possibility. Plans were thwarted, danger mounted and you kept your head. No matter what.

But finding herself in a grungy little cabin with Frankie nowhere to be seen was a surprise she hadn't seen coming.

She'd expected to be taken right to that compound, but it was Granger's words that had been causing her to rethink that there in the back of that car.

Give them what they expect.

Frankie had known what they would expect, and he'd done the opposite. It made her blood run cold. If he knew enough to surprise them…

She couldn't finish that thought. She looked at the men in the room with them. Three inside. Likely the others remained on guard outside. All armed with tactical gear, big guns and nasty sneers on their faces.

She glanced at Granger without moving her head.

Like her, he was studying the surroundings. But he didn't look at her, not even in his peripheral vision.

She studied his head wound. He'd bled through the bandage and his face and beard were caked with dried blood. How much longer would he be able to push through that? How much longer—

Get it together, Shay.

She had wanted to come on this mission alone because she didn't want anyone she cared about hurt, and because she truly did believe this was *her* deal. Her penance.

But beyond those very real, complex feelings of guilt and blame, there was this. She didn't know how to maintain her old brick wall. When she hadn't cared overly much if she or anyone else lived or died. She'd been an operative, and each mission had been about the end goal. Not about life and death.

But she'd lost that. Somewhere between the day of the explosion at the old headquarters and the day Granger had told her he was entrusting North Star to her.

And she'd known, last month when Vianni's men had been closing in, that she couldn't access that old part of herself. It was gone. Dissolved somehow.

Maybe it had been an insult to Granger and the rest of North Star to not use their skills, but she didn't know how to be the kind of leader Granger had always been.

And *this* was why. She was thinking about him

and Elsie and everyone else rather than what they needed to do to get out of this predicament.

Unfortunately, there was no escaping this cabin. Maybe she and Granger could fight off the men, knowing the men wouldn't shoot to kill, but then what? It didn't get them what they wanted: an end to this.

And Frankie knew. He had to know that was their ultimate goal.

So, what was his?

Not her dead. He could have done that long before she'd known he was still alive. Or at least, his end goal wasn't her dead without playing some games first. Frankie loved his games. He wanted her to pay for deceiving him, leaving him behind to die.

So, he'd want her to be afraid. Terrified. Hurt and devastated. But not dead. Not yet.

Would he understand what she was most afraid of? Would he have any concept of the woman she'd become? How could he? And if he still thought of her as that shallow, confused girl who'd wanted excitement, but not quite the getting knocked around and told what to do kind, what did he think she was afraid of?

She took a deep breath in an effort to calm her circling thoughts. They were good questions, but she needed to take it one step at a time. Not get overwhelmed by all the possibilities.

If she could get into the same room as Frankie, see him face-to-face, listen to what he had to say—

no matter how many lies or fake stories he offered—
she might be able to figure it out. What he wanted.
What he expected.

And if she could do that, she could make this work
in her favor. She had no other choice. Everyone she
loved was on the line.

She looked at the three men inside. One of them
had to be a leader or commander of some kind—the
direct communicator to Frankie. She studied the one
by the door. He mostly looked straight ahead, holding the gun close to his body. He didn't aim it, but
he was ready to shoot if he needed to.

But not her. He wasn't supposed to shoot her.

This time, she didn't let herself look at Granger.
She looked at the other two men. They both stood
at windows on opposite sides of the cabin, standing
in the exact same position the guy by the door was.

Door guy wouldn't be the commander she was
looking for. If something happened, he'd need to go
out. He'd need to be the first one to act. So, it would
be one of the window guys.

Shay watched them for a while, waiting for *something* to distinguish one of them. She wasn't sure how
long she waited. The frustration of standing there silently waiting for *something* made time stand still.
But, when one glanced at the watch on his wrist, and
she looked over at the other who didn't have a watch,
she figured she'd found her man.

She looked right at him, waiting till his gaze
swept around the room and landed on her staring at

him. He didn't measure any surprise that she'd ze-roed in on him, just held her gaze. Blankly.

"So, when do I get to have a tearful reunion with my supposedly dead husband?"

The man stared back at her. He didn't sneer or snicker like the men who'd led her there had. Maybe he hadn't been one of them, or maybe she just hadn't noticed one being quiet.

But that made her sure she'd targeted the right man.

"We just gonna stand around in silence? Let me tell you, as torture goes that's not quite the method I'd use."

Still, he didn't move or say anything.

Shay had to bite her tongue to keep herself from demanding something—anything. Standing there still and silent *was* a kind of torture.

She clenched her hands into fists and bit her tongue and waited. The silence was oppressive. The stand-ing painful after so many injuries along the way. She wanted to fight. She wanted to yell. She wanted to—

Then she heard the faint slam of a car door. Watched as all the guards exchanged looks and the man at the door nodded and then slipped out.

The head guy looked at her and finally showed some semblance of being something other than a robot. He smiled. "Might want to pretty yourself up, sweetheart. Here comes the husband."

Shay didn't turn and look at the door. She didn't register surprise or fear or anything else. Instead, she kept her breathing even and imagined that she was encased in some kind of ice chamber. Still, frozen in place and utterly uninterested in anything around her.

She couldn't give *anything* away to Frankie, because likely *anything* could get someone she cared about dead.

GRANGER WATCHED SHAY still herself. She'd already been standing still, but relaxed. Everything in her tensed until she was like a statue. Not rigid or tense. Simply impenetrable.

Impressive. Granger tried to mimic it. But he hadn't expected Frankie to come *here*. He'd expected a long wait and some mind games before they were taken to the main compound. The *nice* compound, with all the trappings of wealth Frankie Vianni liked to surround himself with to feel important.

Granger didn't like how the man kept surprising them.

He heard the door behind him open, but he didn't turn to look and see if it was the guard returning or the devil himself. He stared straight ahead in an at-ease position reminding himself he'd dealt with worse than Frankie.

Ace Wyatt who'd once run the Sons of the Badlands, who'd been responsible for Anna's death in a more *actual* way than Frankie, had been bigger, slicker, meaner than Frankie.

Of course, he'd also been insane and fancied himself some kind of god.

Frankie didn't have that. He was just vicious, and smart enough to make the people around him pay if they didn't fall in line.

"Well, well, well." His voice hadn't changed, but Granger didn't turn his head. A surreptitious look to Shay showed him the same. She looked straight ahead, expression blank and military-esque.

Frankie took his time. He didn't appear in front of them for a while, as if waiting them out. Trying to get them to turn their heads to look at him.

He finally gave up the wait and came to stand in front of them. And it was definitely not the Frankie Vianni Granger remembered.

He'd bulked up, for starters. No longer tall and wiry in an elegant suit. He was a tall, muscular man who sported a dark beard now, looking more the Idaho wilderness survivor man than suave Chicago gangster.

A wiggle of dread tried to break through Granger's composure, but he didn't let it. He'd done a little survivor man-ing himself.

Frankie studied them with shrewd eyes. His father had been a sledgehammer. Too heavy-handed, too certain in his power. Where the original Vianni family had wreaked havoc as dirty law enforcement, the next generation had made the kind of mistakes that had gotten the original generation put behind bars, their control over the police department evaporating all because of Gio Vianni's blunders.

But Gio had managed to stay out of prison. He'd managed to make his family look on the up-and-up, while Frankie had taken after grandpa and built a brand new empire.

Granger knew the family dynamics. Anna had explained them to him in no uncertain terms. Gio might have been the figurehead of the Vianni family, but Frankie had been the brains behind their resurrection.

Frankie Vianni was smart. Cruel and vicious, sure, but clever. He'd always made a point of separating himself from the family business so the law couldn't touch him. While pulling all the strings.

And when he'd finally failed at that, he'd faked his own death.

That one still stuck in Granger's craw. Anna was dead and this weasel had managed to live. Over and over again, no matter how many people wanted him dead.

Granger himself included.

But he had learned something since he'd been shot and burned. Revenge was sweet, sure, but it also blinded. It warped what his mission should always be: stop a monster like Frankie from hurting more innocent people.

So, he couldn't think about Anna or what Frankie deserved. He had to cool off the red-hot anger deep inside of him. Had to remain calm and collected thinking about getting Shay out of this mess.

She might have married this man willingly, but she'd been a young girl who hadn't known what she'd been getting herself into. If there was any blame, no doubt ten years as a North Star operative was penance enough.

"An interesting duo," Frankie was saying, studying them both. "My wife. My brother-in-law. A little piece of Chicago, right here in the Idaho wilderness."

"Oh, is that where we are?" Shay asked, pretending like he'd given something away even though Granger was well aware they all knew they were in Idaho.

Frankie only smiled. "You've gotten more clever, Veronica. I'll admit, I've been surprised at your development. I always figured you were the kind of stupid even a man like me couldn't fix."

Shay didn't take the bait. She shrugged negligently.

"And it seems you've worked out not just your mind, but your body," he said silkily, moving closer to her.

Granger had to curl his hands into fists to remind himself to stay where he was. Even as Frankie came to stand right in front of Shay, giving her a slow, disgusting once-over.

She stood her ground, appearing to all unaffected by the blatant perusal.

Frankie reached out and tapped her cheek with

his index finger and Granger had to breathe through the red haze of *violence* that swept through him. It wasn't an overtly sexual or threatening gesture, and somehow that made it worse.

"You'll do quite well, wife," Frankie said. Then his gaze slid to Granger.

Frankie studied him critically, and Granger kept his face perfectly placid. Even as primal fury tried to wage war inside of him.

"I'll admit, I've never been able to completely figure this out." He gestured from Shay to him and back again. "Guilt? Revenge? Why'd you help her? When you had to know she was involved in all sorts of dastardly plans of mine."

Granger didn't say anything, and neither did Shay. They were definitely on the same page. Don't give Frankie anything he could use against them—words, emotions, reactions.

"Of course, that's a silly question isn't it?" Frankie said with a little laugh, his gaze fully on Granger now. "You knew Anna was involved in things and you looked the other way."

It was a shock that Frankie knew that, but maybe because he'd just admitted the same to Shay, it didn't hit like the blow it was meant to be. Granger was able to keep his reaction under the surface. Giving Frankie nothing.

"Admirable restraint, Agent Macmillan. *Admirable*." He tilted his head to one side, studying Granger with a patient, searching gaze that didn't bode well. Then he smiled. "But we'll break you yet."

SABRINA KILLIAN DID not do *almost-died* recovery well. She pushed herself too hard. She snapped at anyone who dared tell her so. Including her boyfriend, who somehow still put up with her. Still managed to love her, no matter how much of a jerk she was.

Connor Lindstrom *might* be superhuman, not that she'd ever admit that to him. Especially when he was off helping Shay face her past and she was stuck here with Froggy, his S&R dog, while everyone else got to be out there in the fray.

"I'm not *that* injured anymore," she muttered to the dog, who had her head resting on Sabrina's lap, sleeping on the couch…where Sabrina wasn't supposed to let her sleep, but had been whenever Connor was out on a mission.

So *maybe* she had a soft spot for dogs. Sue her.

Her phone vibrated in her pocket and she answered it in a rush, hoping Connor had good news to impart. "Hey, how's it going?"

There was a pause. Not a long one, but enough of one.

She swallowed, trying to keep the fear out of her voice. "That bad?"

"We've lost track of them," Connor said matter-of-factly. "But Elsie's working on it."

"Lost track. Connor, that's not just bad that's a

dis…" She trailed off as the dog half in her lap snuffled in her sleep. "Froggy can track them," she said.

"Yes, Froggy can track them. We don't want to lose our numbers here when everything is so up in the air, so…"

Sabrina practically jumped to her feet, waking up Froggy in the process. "I'll bring her."

"Yes, but you listen to me, Killian," he said sternly. "You are still on the injured list, you understand that? You're *just* bringing Froggy. That's *it*."

"You're adorable."

"Sabrina."

His voice was grave, and because she knew him she could tell he was tired and worried, and adding worry about her wasn't going to make him feel any better.

But he had to understand… "It's Shay."

"I know." He let out a long sigh. "Bring Froggy. Her gear and… Hell, bring yours too, but you're the *last* resort, Sabrina. Promise me you understand that."

"Yeah, yeah, yeah. I'll be there soon."

"Be careful. I love you."

He always said it with such *conviction*, even all these months later it hit her a little hard.

"Love you too," she muttered, which made him laugh. She'd never understand why, or maybe it was simply because he understood her and how that was still a strange, humbling thing for her to admit out loud to anyone, least of all routinely.

But she hung up the phone and looked at the dog. "Well, Froggy, we've got a mission. This one is important. You're going to find Shay for us."

And Sabrina was going to help bring her home.

Chapter Thirteen

Revulsion pooled in Shay's stomach. Once upon a time, she'd fancied herself in love with the man in front of her. Because he'd made her nervous, and all her friends had always giggled about boys who gave them butterflies. Because he'd paid attention to her and bought her presents when all her friends had complained their boyfriends wouldn't even take them to McDonald's and pay.

She knew she'd been young and sheltered and Frankie had targeted her because she was pretty and he fancied her dumb and weak enough to be the kind of woman who'd fit well on his arm. There were excuses she could make herself feel better with, sure.

But faced with the reality of the situation, she could only feel sick to her stomach over how stupid she'd been.

Still, that didn't change her current situation.

And Frankie was right. She'd changed. Gotten smarter and stronger, and she could feel ill over that young woman making bad choices, but *this* woman wasn't going to repeat those mistakes.

This woman had learned how to fight, thanks to the man standing next to her, and that's what she was going to do.

She had to be careful about what she said and how she said it, but she couldn't stand Frankie's attention on Granger. So, she broke her silence.

"So, Frank," she said, knowing he'd hated that because it had been his grandfather's name, and he blamed his grandfather for all the work he'd had to do to rebuild the Vianni name.

Even though it had been his father who'd made the mistakes that had gotten Frank thrown in jail, where he'd died.

"I know I was a great catch and all, but this seems like an awful lot of work to get back a wife who clearly didn't want you."

Like she'd hoped, his attention turned back to her. He smiled, that cruel smile that had her stomach cramping, and a muscle memory wanting her to flinch and brace herself for a blow.

She managed to fight back the flinch, but it was a near thing.

"Oh, it wasn't so clear, was it, Veronica? You wanted me well enough."

Another roll of nausea went through her, but she held his dark gaze. "I think you have me confused with one of your prostitutes."

He let out a little tinkle of a laugh as though she

had a delightful sense of humor. "You always could make me laugh, Veronica. It was a shame you were so stupid. We could have done great things together."

The sad thing was, when she'd been eighteen, she'd believed him. That she was stupid. That everything that went wrong was her fault. Luckily, she wasn't eighteen anymore.

"So," he said conversationally, walking away from her and Granger and toward the door. She didn't let her gaze follow him. She went back to looking forward at the wall.

"When do you think your friends will be arriving?"

Terror gripped her in a new way. *Your friends.* He meant North Star. And if he was bringing it up…

That meant he'd set a trap for North Star. Even though he had her, he wanted to hurt them too. She kept her breathing even, but it was a fight. No matter what Frankie's plans were, she couldn't panic, though God, she felt it pulsing through her.

Frankie couldn't see it. So, she forced herself to just breathe.

Granger cleared his throat, almost inaudibly. She looked at him. He didn't say anything, but she understood his expression well enough. It was like when he'd told her it was an insult not to use their skills to help her.

Those people out there who wanted to help her weren't weak and helpless. She didn't think they were, but something about fear made them all too mortal. And this situation was so fully hers, it would

always be a blame on her own shoulders if someone got hurt.

She knew, she *knew* she couldn't think about all
the people out there who could die, what it would
mean to their families. She *knew* that and yet the
panic wound through her tighter and tighter.

When this was *her* mess, and she didn't have anyone waiting for her. She didn't have a family anymore. No one to need her. No one to love her.

Except all those people out there.

Shay felt like crying. Partly because it was
Granger's voice in her head, reminding her that just
as she loved the people who'd become like her sur-
rogate family, they loved her in return. If she could
get past her own hang-ups, put herself in their shoes,
she'd be doing the same damn thing.

"This isn't where they thought we'd be," Granger
said under his breath. As if that was new information. Even though it wasn't, it broke her out of the
circular panic whirl of her thoughts.

She frowned at him, but didn't have time to work
through him saying aloud what they both already
knew.

"What was that?" Frankie asked. Since they'd refused to look back at him, he'd returned to stand before them. He studied Granger's face. "What did you
just try to whisper to her?"

Granger shrugged and offered Frankie a bland
smile. "You must be hearing things, Frank."

Quick as a snake, Frankie reached out and

punched Granger in the face. Granger's head jerked to the side with the force of the blow, but he immediately turned it back so he could look at Frankie. Other than the head move, he reacted not at all. Not a grunt, not a flinch, not even a bunching of muscles like he was preparing to fight back.

"I can make it hurt," Frankie seethed.

"I'm sure you can. Have your men hold me down, point their guns at me. You can inflict all kinds of damage, big man that you are. Kicking a man who can't fight back."

Frankie's expression went mutinous, but he held himself still. He'd curled his hands into fists as he sneered at Granger, breathing just a little bit too heavily.

Granger was trying to goad him into acting, into making a mistake, but after tense, silent minutes Frankie carefully got himself back under control. He didn't throw another punch, didn't order his men away.

He smiled at Granger. "I don't underestimate you, Macmillan. You're good at what you do." He stepped closer, so they were toe to toe, eye to eye. "But I'm better."

Granger shrugged negligently. "Guess we'll find out."

"We certainly will." He nodded to someone behind them. Then Granger was grabbed roughly from behind.

Shay couldn't prevent herself from reaching out.

An instinct to stop everything. Granger shook his head and let the man drag him to the door.

But separating them was awful. What would they do to Granger?

And it was too soon. North Star would need some time to follow them. To figure out where they were. They needed more time. This was terrible.

Meant to be terrible. She looked at Frankie and he was grinning at her.

"Say goodbye, Veronica. It might be your last chance."

GRANGER LET HIMSELF be dragged. His heart beat a little too hard in his chest because likely more pain was coming. Possibly worse than that.

He'd fight it, but if Frankie ordered one of his men to shoot him in the head, that was pretty much it. North Star might be able to find them eventually, but even they would need more time.

If his time was up, his time was up. He could accept that. Maybe not from Frankie or one of his goons, but you put yourself in danger enough times you got a little fatalistic about death.

But what really bugged him was that Shay would spend the rest of her life blaming herself if he ended up dead right now. So, he had to think.

The guard pushed him outside where he was grabbed by another one. The original guard went back in, but Frankie soon emerged from the ramshackle cabin.

He didn't speak to his guard, and the guard didn't ask any questions. Whatever this was had been planned in advance.

Granger tried to predict what it might be. Some kind of torture—physical or emotional—as revenge for raiding his family, taking them down…or at least forcing the Viannis to fake their own deaths and go into hiding?

It just didn't gel. The problem was, nothing really did.

The guard gave him a shove and Granger narrowly missed plowing into a tree since his hands were bound behind him, but he somehow managed to keep his balance and merely bounce into the rough bark.

The guard roughly whirled him around, so now his back was to the tree and he was facing Frankie, who stood in front of him dressed all in black, hands clasped behind his back. He wore no weapons. Wasn't in a fighting stance. Instead, he simply stood and watched.

Waiting.

But for *what*?

"It's been fascinating watching you work the past few years," Frankie said casually. Then smirked. "Or not work, as the case may be in those early days of your recovery. I hope you've got those dogs and horses somewhere safe."

Granger had dealt with enough men who wanted to terrify him to know how to keep his game face, but the fact Frankie knew about his ranch and his animals was a shock. He didn't let it show, but he knew he didn't have quite the pithy response that would have shown the bastard just how unaffected he was.

Because he *was* affected. Even knowing his animals were in good hands. He'd moved the dogs to the Bluebird Inn and his horses to a neighboring ranch. Vianni men could burn down his place—it wouldn't make a difference. They wouldn't get what they were after.

And Granger doubted very much he was meant to live past this interaction with Frankie Vianni, so what did threatening him with things he'd never see again matter?

Even if it did make him sick to his stomach, Frankie had clearly kept tabs on him. When they'd been so careful. When they'd managed to be a secret for so long.

Something had happened in the past few months. Somehow, the Viannis had gotten through. Granger didn't know how. Elsie would have been able to see a security breech in their tech. And they didn't take on very many new people, certainly not without thorough background checks, especially after what had happened two years ago.

Two years ago…

Frankie had said for the past *years*.

Granger's mind whirled with the possibility that Frankie had been planning something for *two* years while North Star worked, fully ending the Sons and taking down corrupt military officials and weapons dealers.

Thinking that the Vianni threat had been eradicated completely. Because they hadn't known there were still some Viannis out there. Lying in wait.

"My Veronica did an admirable job running your little vigilante group, didn't she? I mean, she didn't take down any gangs like the great Granger Macmillan, but she held her own. Impressive. Surprising, really. I didn't think she had it in her."

Granger laughed. "You don't know her at all." At least, he was going to do everything in his power to make Frankie think he didn't. Because it was better for Vianni to keep underestimating her.

"It appears I didn't, but deep down, Veronica is the same girl I knew. I was married to her. We shared a bed, Macmillan." Frankie smirked. "I know her well enough. And I know that the only reason she managed anything in the decade since you took her away is that she had a strong male lead to follow. To admire. To look up to, among other things."

Granger had to weigh his words. Be careful to make it sound like he was speaking out of spite or anger, rather than the truth. So Frankie believed he would let this all slip because Frankie had gotten the better of him. Because his side innuendos had effected him.

And maybe they had enough that his words would sound truthful when it wasn't the truth at all. "You remember a young woman you knocked around and manipulated, but I saved her from that. I taught her how to be a leader. How to separate her emotions from the task at hand. And then I left her in the lurch. We might work together well enough, but I'm no hero to her anymore."

Frankie made a considering noise. "Well, I'll give you one thing, she doesn't have much loyalty. She took her sister-in-law's husband at the drop of the hat, didn't she?"

Granger wanted to deny it—defend both Anna's memory and give Shay more credit, but it didn't matter what Frankie thought. The truth didn't matter here.

"You're no hero to her, but I'm betting the people who work for her are *something* to her. Why else would she try to keep them out of this? It was kind of you to bring them in. Much easier on me."

Granger didn't say anything. Agreements or denials would both hurt here. So, he simply did what he'd done in the cabin. Kept his mouth shut and looked straight ahead, carefully devoid of any emotion.

Frankie looked back at the cabin. "You know, I always thought you and I weren't so different. It was why Anna played both sides. You and your DEA cronies trying to take me down, the Vianni family trying to do the same right back."

Granger tried to look horrified, since that was what Frankie so clearly wanted. "It isn't the same," he said, adding some rasp to his voice.

"Isn't it? Weren't you just me with the law behind you?"

It hurt, even though he knew it wasn't true. He also knew there was *some* truth to it. Because he'd bent laws, and done things he shouldn't have in the pursuit of justice. Or vengeance. Depending on the day.

"You let that one sink in for a while. Because lucky for you, I don't want you dead just yet."

And *that* was terrifying.

HOLDEN PARKER STOOD in a snowbank next to Connor Lindstrom. What had once been a suspicious and perhaps edgy distrust of one another had grown into something more of a friendship, if only because Sabrina insisted…and Connor was a sap over the woman Holden had always seen as a sister.

But that was why Holden was currently rather irritated with his friend. "I don't like it."

Connor shrugged, eyeing the white horizon. "You think I do?"

"She's not going to go back to headquarters once she's here."

"No, she isn't," Connor agreed.

Which was irritating. The guy never did want to *fight* or *bicker*, unlike Sabrina, who was always up for a good fight. And shouldn't be coming into this one. "Someone else couldn't have brought your dog?"

"Not as quickly since she was with my dog."

"I don't get why we need the dog anyway. Why Elsie is cutting off actual tech that will get us what we want." Of course, Holden did know. He just didn't like the reason. Because if their computer genius was telling them not to use their computers and comm units, that meant someone else was.

Connor didn't say anything to that. Holden supposed Connor knew he was complaining to pass the time not because he was that stupid.

"You think she'd marry me?" Connor asked. Completely and utterly out of the blue.

Holden didn't think much could surprise him anymore, but this sure did… "Huh?"

"You know her better than anyone. Or understand her better than anyone. She's not traditional. She's not…anything. So I'm asking, do you think she'd get to the point where she'd do something as traditional as marry me?"

Holden blinked and studied the man next to him. Connor kept his gaze on the horizon, his expression placid, but there was a tenseness inside of him that belied his calm demeanor.

And since Connor was anxious enough over his answer no matter how little he wanted to show it, Holden considered the question.

He did understand Sabrina better than most. They'd had similar views on life, though they often expressed them in different ways. His marriage to Willa had changed his outlook, and he figured that for Sabrina, those old views could change too. Now that she'd found Connor.

"The thing about Sabrina is… She grew up tough. She never really had anyone who loved her, not the way parents and family are supposed to anyway. Sabrina gave everything to the SEALs and then she's too injured to see that through. She's had tough break after tough break, but *she* didn't break."

"I know all that."

"I know you do, but my point here is that… It's not about being traditional or not. It's about not knowing what to do with it. Love and family and all that. North Star and you, it helps, but she's not going to know what to do with a marriage proposal. She might not even say yes, but deep down, Sabrina wants what everyone wants. A place to belong, people to love her. People she loves back. Traditional or not, marriage is the promise of that. It might freak her out at first, but yeah, I think she'd eventually say yes. Because though you do a better job of hiding it, you're as stubborn and obnoxious as she is."

Connor let out a little huff of a laugh. "Why does that sound like a compliment coming from you?"

"Because it is." Holden gave Connor's shoulder a little shove. "You're all right, Lindstrom."

"Yeah, you too," Connor muttered. He pointed toward the west. "They're coming."

Holden had been an operative for a long time, but Connor's ex-SEAL and S&R training never failed to impress him. Because in another minute, Sabrina and Connor's dog appeared at the crest of the hill.

She sauntered down the hill toward them, though Holden wasn't fooled. That saunter was meant to hide her limp.

"Don't you two make quite a pair," she said as she approached with one of her trademark devil-may-care grins. But it didn't hide the tense set of her jaw, likely against the pain she had to be in.

"Aren't you supposed to still be using a cane?" Holden asked, smiling right back though it was a desperate attempt not to shake some sense into her.

"Betty cleared me to walk on my own last week, thank you very much."

"So, you thought you'd hike cross-country?"

Her gaze moved from Holden to Connor. "What have you got to say?"

He leaned in and gave her a quick kiss. "I'm glad to see you."

She blinked, and Holden realized Connor really was perfect for her because he could put aside all the concerns and fears he had about her health, and play her like a fiddle.

She scowled at her boyfriend, then at Holden. "Listen, I know my limitations. But it's Shay. It's Granger. I'm not going to get myself killed doing something stupid, but I'm damn well going to be out here doing what I can to bring them home."

Connor slid his arm over her shoulders and they

both looked at Holden, the dog happily wagging its tail between them.

She gave Holden a smirk. "See, I can be reasonable."

He didn't bother to respond. "So, what's the plan?"

"Connor and Froggy will do their best to get a lead on Shay or Granger. Hopefully they're together, but if we get one, Elsie and her paper map can work on the other, hopefully. Holden and I will stay here and man the analog radio. If Connor needs backup, you'll go after him. Elsie's got a whole radio compound set up."

"Did she say what's wrong with the computer and comm systems from this century?" Holden asked.

Sabrina frowned and shook her head. "No. She was a little preoccupied trying to get everything set up without it."

Fair enough.

"When you find them, or even get a good, reliable idea of what direction they went in, you hold. You don't act. From everything we can tell we've got time, so we need to do this right. You radio your location and we go from there."

Connor nodded. "Promise me you're going to stay put and man the radios?" Before Sabrina could say *anything*, Connor fixed her with a steely glare. "Promise."

To Holden's surprise, she winkled her nose. "Fine," she muttered. "I promise unless there are extraordinary circumstances."

Connor rolled his eyes, but he apparently wasn't going to argue with her. "All right. Well, while you do that, why don't you think about marrying me?" He leaned in, kissed her soundly on the mouth, then began to walk away while Sabrina watched him go, her expression one of pure and utter shock.

Holden had to grin. He'd never seen her so taken aback, and he'd known her a long time.

"He's not serious," she muttered, but she didn't move. And she didn't stop staring at Connor's quickly disappearing form.

"Seems to be," Holden replied.

Sabrina whipped her head around and glared at him. "But…why?"

Holden reached out, gave her shoulder a little squeeze. "Bad news. I think he loves you, Sabrina."

She scowled at him and whacked his hand away. "Well, I know that."

"Love does funny things to people. Has them thinking about normalcy and not carrying around high-profile weapons through the mountains and woods trying to take down the bad guys."

"Sounds terrible." But she didn't sound so convinced. "How normal are you feeling these days?"

Holden rocked back on his heels. He scanned the area around them as he'd been doing since he and Connor had decided this was a good meeting spot. No sign of Vianni's men or the other North Star groups patrolling the area. They were far enough out no one should stumble upon them, but he kept a lookout.

And he decided he might as well be honest with Sabrina. If only to help her toward seeing marriage wasn't quite so crazy a thought. "Willa and I are thinking about having a kid."

"You're…*what*?"

"Not quite there yet, but getting there. Lianna walking around with that tiny baby is really doing a number on my wife."

"Your wife."

"Yeah, still weird."

"You love it."

"I do. I love her. And you know, I'm kinda growing to love the farm stuff too. There's something about living without feeling like there's a target on your back or someone to take down that just…sits okay. I could maybe live my life with a little less animal waste, but all in all, Willa makes up for it."

Sabrina's eyebrows were furrowed, and she still watched where Connor and his dog had disappeared. She held the radio in her hand.

Holden figured she wasn't going to say anything else, so he fiddled with the old-fashioned radio walkie Elsie had managed to get distributed to everyone. It would be tougher to communicate cross groups, and wasn't nearly as stealthy, but at least they'd be able to talk to Elsie.

"Search and rescue isn't so bad," Sabrina said into the silence after a while.

Holden looked down at her. She was staring straight ahead, to where Connor had disappeared. She had a line between her eyes like she was frowning even though her expression was placid.

"No, I don't suppose it is," he agreed.

"Connor's an okay pilot, and I'm an excellent tracker. Of course, we'd have to hire on some help if we wanted to start an S&R group. Obviously only if the North Star work ever dried up."

"Obviously. What kind of help?"

Sabrina shrugged. "More trackers. Some admin staff. That sort of thing." She finally looked up at him. "It's helping people without the target on your back."

And he realized that in the months since he'd "semiretired" from North Star, that's exactly what he'd been looking for. A way to do good without putting his life on the line, time and time again. Because he wanted to go home to his wife and, yeah, start a family.

Leave it to Sabrina to find a way to offer them that. He cleared his throat, looked away from her and to the white world around them. Like old times. Old missions. But maybe, *hopefully*, the last one. "But first, we help Shay and Granger."

"Yeah, just like they helped us once upon a time."

Chapter Fourteen

When Frankie returned, Shay refused to demand where Granger was, though that's what she most wanted to do. But he wanted that desperation from her. He wanted her to fall into a blubbering mess at his feet. Frankie wanted her scared and desperate.

She thought about it. After all, weren't they a little bit giving him what he wanted? Playing into the way he thought they should act so they could take him off guard?

Shay looked at him, opened her mouth to say something deferential or pleading, but no words came out. She ordered herself to swallow her pride, though every part of her fought against it.

Then she thought back to what she'd been allowed to observe as her position as Frankie's wife. Nothing too important, but she'd once seen a man beg for his life. Frankie had gotten a lot of enjoyment out of that.

But he'd still killed the guy. Not in *front* of Shay, and maybe not even by his own hand, but she'd known—he'd made sure she knew—the man had wound up dead the very next day.

Had she ever seen anyone change Frankie's point of view? Anyone alter his plans? Not that she could remember, but sometimes he would act impulsively. And when he did that, he'd usually make a mistake.

It wasn't easy to get to that impulsive side of Frankie. He knew his own weaknesses and he ruthlessly tried to eradicate them. Likely, he'd gotten even better at it in the decade since she'd been married to him.

But didn't it make sense in the present to do all she could to enflame his temper? To try to get to that point where he made a mistake. Maybe he expected her to fall apart and beg, but wouldn't it fluster him more if she didn't?

Sure, it was risky. He could impulsively *kill* her or Granger, and then where would she be?

But maybe, if she poked the right places, it could end up showing a crack in his armor. Maybe she could get *somewhere* that would help them escape this if she made him really, *really* mad.

In Shay's estimation, it was worth the effort. But before she could try, to her surprise, one of the guards pulled Granger back inside the cabin. He was shoved roughly inside, but not left to stand next to Shay like before. They jerked his arms in separate directions and cuffed him to two hooks in the wall.

She searched his face for signs of new injury, but the blood seemed to be old from his head wound from the crash, and he didn't look any worse for the wear.

What *was* this?

"We'll play a little game," Frankie said, almost cheerfully.

Shay had to look away from Granger, had to ignore her own fear and remember her new objective. She sighed heavily. "A game? Really? Can't you just get this over with? Hurt us if you want. Kill us if you're going to. Why the drama?"

Frankie's eyes narrowed, but his smile didn't dim. "We've all got to find our own fun somewhere."

"Leave it to you for your 'somewhere' to be cliché villain in a sitcom." She blew out a long, bored breath. "All right. What's this dastardly game you want to play?"

Frankie's jaw set, but he wasn't falling for the bait. "We have a little discussion. You tell the truth and all is well," he said, but she could hear the tension in his voice. "You don't, then your hero here breaks a bone." He wasn't getting the enjoyment of messing with her when she acted unimpressed. When she poked at his pride and his ego.

So, she poked harder.

"Must feel real good having to chain him to a wall to have to hurt him. *Woo* boy, what a tough guy."

Frankie whirled on her. He didn't strike and he didn't say anything, but his breath came in short puffs and she knew she was getting to him. Fifty-

fifty chance it was a mistake, but it was a really *gratifying* mistake.

Granger even laughed, and that *really* set Frankie off.

"Would you prefer I hurt you?" he asked, and she remembered that silky, dangerous tone of voice so well a part of her recoiled. That old, scared part of herself wanted to drop his gaze.

But she wasn't Veronica any longer. She'd built herself into Shay. A woman who wasn't afraid. Who led missions. Who risked her life to save others. "Are you going to leave me cuffed? Because that's not a fair fight."

Frankie burst out laughing. "You think if I took off your cuffs, you could *take* me?"

"No," she replied gravely. "I *know* I could."

"Shay," Granger muttered, a warning. Maybe for show. Maybe not. Shay found she didn't care in the moment. She didn't care about much besides getting the chance to punch Frankie in the face.

She didn't look at Granger. She held Frankie's furious gaze. Chin lifted. Challenge between them.

"You're strong. A fighter now?" Frankie said, his voice low and lethal before he let out another little laugh. This one sharp and mean. "Sending your minions off to do your dirty work for you?"

"Is that what I do?" Shay replied, and she wasn't sure how much the smugness she imbued in her voice and expression was an act and how much was just *there*, because no matter how many insecurities she had about herself as a leader, sending off her minions wasn't one of them. "Must have learned from you."

Frankie's eyes narrowed, but his voice remained that silky threat. "How many of your operatives have been hurt in the past few months? It seems like an awful lot. And yet here you are, unscathed."

She tried not to let her frown show. Frankie said *unscathed* like he didn't know about her gunshot wound, but it had been inflicted by one of his men. He was aware of all the injuries her team had suffered elsewhere. How could her own injury have escaped his unnerving breadth of knowledge about everything that had gone on with North Star the past few months?

But she watched him, not saying anything, and his gaze dipped for a momentary, almost unnoticeable second to the place where she'd been shot.

Could it be that he was *pretending* not to know?

"Well, let's see what you got." He shrugged out of his jacket like he was going to…fight her.

She looked at the men on either side of her. Then at Frankie, standing there as if ready for a boxing match. "You can't be serious."

He nodded at his guards. "Take her cuffs off."

She watched as the guards exchanged confused looks. "Uh, boss…"

They said it in the same uncertain, warning kind of way that Granger growled her name from his spot chained to the wall.

"Take them off," Frankie ordered, the three words

sounding more like a snap of temper than a man in control.

Shay didn't really think she was going to get a chance to fight Frankie. Surely…this was some kind of trick. But with the cuffs off, she got into a fighting stance. "It's hard to believe you're going to let this be a fair fight, Frank."

"You think I'm afraid of you?" he demanded. "They'll stay back. I'll even give you a free sh—"

She hit him before he got the word out of his mouth. It was probably stupid, but she also knew he didn't actually expect her to do it. To be able to hurt him.

And God, she wanted to hurt him. She landed a sharp elbow into his gut and swung it upward to his his nose. He pitched backward on a yelp of pain so she kicked out, a hard rap meant to *really* hurt.

When his guards didn't immediately jump to pull her off Frankie, she *really* let it fly. Shay wanted him on the ground so she could pound into him, so she focused on that end result. She kicked, swept out her legs, punched when she thought he was dodging her other blows too well.

He managed to get in a few of his own. Decent punches, strong and with that follow-through that had sent her sprawling once upon a time.

But she hadn't known how to block or fight back then. *Now*, she did. And she realized he'd allowed this fight to happen because he knew about her injury. He kept aiming for it. Trying to land a blow where she'd been shot.

She didn't let him. She angled her body, protected her bad side, and landed blow after blow that he only minimally dodged.

Get him on his back. Get him on his back… It was the chant in her head, but no matter how many punches and kicks she got in, he just wouldn't go down. He got one good shot, and it hurt no doubt, but luckily landed far enough above her wound that it didn't send her to her knees.

"Enough!" Frankie yelled. He didn't run away or anything. He didn't stop trying to hit her, but pretty soon she was grabbed roughly by the two guards. She would have whirled on them too, but she still wanted Frankie on the ground under her. So she kept going after him.

Her own mistake.

The guards pulled her off and roughly cuffed her again. Frankie grabbed his jacket off the floor with his back to her. He was breathing heavily and he put the garment back on with sharp, frustrated movements. When he turned to face her, he straightened his jacket, sneering at her and seething with rage. Blood dribbled from his nose and mouth. His eye was puffy and he looked to be putting more weight on one leg.

Shay grinned at him. "How's it feel? Trying to pick on someone who can fight right back this go around?"

He wiped the blood from his mouth with the back of his hand. He was vibrating with a rage he couldn't control. "You'll pay for that."

She had no doubt she would.

But it had been worth it.

"YOU KICKED HIS ASS," Granger said in utter surprise. He didn't bother to hush his voice or try to play it cool. He'd kept mostly silent during Shay's fight because…well, he hadn't believed Frankie would let it happen.

But he had. And Granger had only been able to stand there, chained to the wall, in silent awe as Shay had gotten in blow after blow.

Giving Shay the opportunity to do damage had been a mistake on Frankie's part. And he figured she'd known it. She'd poked at his temper until he'd made that mistake.

"Oh, yeah I did," Shay said, with relish.

"Enjoy your childish snickering," Frankie said coolly. His temper strained at the edges. Even Granger could see he was struggling to win the battle against it.

But he was pulling it together. Or trying to. Granger had been a little leery of Shay poking the angry bear, but he'd kept his mouth mostly shut and let her give it a shot. She knew Frankie the best, after all.

And she'd proven herself correct. Proven that she was definitely on the right track.

Shay had hurt Frankie. *Really* laid into him. And that would stick with Frankie, a thorn in his side, for the rest of his life. It made him more dangerous, but it also made him more prone to a stupid mistake like the one he'd just made.

"I can't imagine letting a woman get the better of me," Granger said, and shrugged when Shay glared at him. He was trying to piss Frankie off, not tell the truth. "Especially one I was married to."

"Can you imagine your wife begging for her life? I can. Oh wait, it isn't my imagination, it's a memory. The Sons might have killed Anna, but I was there."

Granger understood this was a "two can play your game" situation. Frankie trying to infuriate him so he'd do something stupid. Granger knew he shouldn't react, shouldn't say anything. But… "She was your sister, man. What the hell is broken inside of you?"

"She was, at best, a liability."

"It doesn't matter," Shay said. "That's the past, and this is today. Frankie, you want to play some more or are you just going to get this over with and kill us? Move on with your life. Because this? This is boring and a waste of your time."

"You're so worried about my time?" he sneered.

"I'm worried about spending my last seconds on earth pretending like I care about anything you have to say."

"Oh, you'll care what I have to say. Because you aren't dying today. In fact, I plan on letting you live a very long time, Veronica. But you will watch everyone you love die."

"Everyone I love can do what I just did to you, Frank."

But Frankie laughed, and he zeroed in on Shay. "Soon enough, your team will find you. They'll track you down. Of course they will. And they will fall into every single trap I've left for them." He tilted his head. "You're not laughing so hard now, Veronica."

"I don't know what would give you the impression you could trick our team," Granger said, having a deep-seated need to keep Frankie's focus off Shay and on him. "Our team took down the Sons. We took down the old guard of Vianni who tried to silence a loose thread. We've always won. Why would now be different?"

Frankie eyed him, and smiled. Not in anger, and that had Granger's heart turning to ice.

"I've been watching you for two years, Macmillan. *Two years.* Since I nearly blew you up." He looked at Shay again. "I have had eyes and ears into every mission you've put together and fought. I know your team, maybe better than you do. And I know exactly what it will take to have them all exactly where I want them."

Granger couldn't help but slide a look at Shay. Her expression was grim, but she wasn't showing that she was afraid, even though Granger knew she was. *He* was.

He'd asked Shay to trust in their skills—his and

North Star and everyone who wanted to help her. Now, he had to trust them too. It was hard. Especially if Frankie had been watching them for *two* years.

But the one thing Frankie couldn't know was that Elsie was listening. And Granger had to believe, hope, *pray*, that it would be the ace in the hole that kept them all from falling into Frankie's trap.

REECE MONTGOMERY HAD been enjoying his retirement, much to the surprise of everyone around him—even his wife, Lianna's, who still every once in a while asked him if he didn't miss it.

He didn't. Maybe it was age. Maybe it was maturity. But mostly it was just finally finding what he'd always wanted. Home. A family.

He didn't relish leaving both behind. Lianna had a lot on her hands with eight-year-old Henry and baby Lark, plus the bed-and-breakfast. She'd hired some help, but that didn't mean Reece relished being away from his family. Even if he was getting more sleep on a mission than he did with a fussy newborn.

Reece looked around at the deep, dark night around him. Frigid cold. No, he didn't miss this.

The other team had gotten Connor's search dog and were tracking Shay and Granger that way, but Reece's team had been given instructions from Elsie that she'd relayed from Granger. They weren't totally clear, so they'd split up to decide which path was best, with Reece standing back as lookout and communications.

Elsie had told him that Frankie Vianni was setting a trap for them. One Vianni expected them to fall into. Presumably so that he could torture Shay by hurting those who'd come to save her.

Reece had no way to get word to his team to be wary of traps. He could only stand here and wait for them to hopefully come back. But, while he waited, he thought about the problem at hand, and he worked up a plan.

One he desperately hoped he wouldn't have to suggest.

The first to return was Cody Wyatt, and though they'd all gone in different directions, Wyatt's brothers weren't far behind. They stood together in silence, waiting for the last member of their team to return. Reece wasn't ready to sound the alarm, but he was watching his clock. He'd give Gabriel Saunders, a North Star operative Reece had worked with quite a bit, another thirty minutes, and then they'd have to act.

The Wyatt brothers on the other hand, he didn't really know. His and Cody's time with North Star had only barely overlapped and they'd been in separate sectors. He'd been on the case when Shay had gone rogue with Tucker, but again, not much contact. He'd never met Jamison Wyatt, and had learned from Elsie he'd only come because Shay had been part of a team that had saved him from an almost deadly run-in with his gang leader of a father.

The same gang Reece's parents had belonged to.

The world was small enough, he supposed, when you dealt in different kinds of revenge.

"Any word on the dog?" Cody asked, coming to stand next to Reece as he rubbed his gloved hands together. They didn't dare risk a fire, but Reece sure wished they could.

He was getting soft, all things considered.

Reece shook his head in response to Cody's question. "Not yet. These analogue communications really slow things down."

"Yeah, hard to track at night too, for everyone. I couldn't see any sign of movement in my quadrant."

"Me neither," Tucker Wyatt added. "But we're talking about a pretty big group of people. Even as dark as it is, they'd have trouble covering up their movements."

"Unless they had someone specifically designated to clean up their movements," Reece replied grimly. He'd worked a few cases like that.

"As long as we're being this timid and this careful, we're always going to be two steps behind, bad communications or not," Jamison Wyatt said.

Reece wished he didn't agree. But sometimes you had to take some risks to have a better chance of coming out on the other end with what you wanted. What would they risk to save Shay and Granger?

"The problem is, Elsie overheard this Vianni guy tell Granger that he's laid some traps for us. And he expects North Star to fall into all of them." Reece looked at the three men around him, shrouded in dark. Though Cody and Tucker had both worked with North Star in some capacity, they were outliers. Either their time with North Star had been brief or a long time ago.

He could only hope that meant they'd tell him that the idea he'd been formulating sucked, and they could continue being careful. Not taking risks.

But how long could they do that before Shay and Granger wound up dead?

"I have an idea, but I'm not so sure it's a great one," Reece said. "It's risky. Possibly riskier than we need it to be. But Shay and Granger allowed themselves to get caught on purpose. While I realize they both knew they were putting themselves in the line of fire to keep others out of it, I also don't think they went in there sure they would die. They had hope they could get themselves out."

"I agree," Cody said grimly. "Shay might have played martyr, but she's too good of an agent just to accept defeat even in sacrifice."

"So, maybe it's not a bad way to go. If this Vianni guy is laying traps for us, why not fall into one?" Reece offered.

There was a careful silence, a *considering* silence, and Reece half wished he'd kept his mouth shut. But he knew…deep down, this was the risk they needed to take. No matter how much he didn't want to take it.

"All of us?" Jamison asked, his voice calm and devoid of emotion.

Reece shook his head. "Not all. I think it's safe

to say Vianni doesn't know about you three. Vera Parker is another outlier. If we send only who he thinks is in North Star, we might be able to fool him."

"You're an outlier too, technically," Cody said, nodding at Reece. "You've been out for a while, right?"

"But not that long."

"Long enough. I know you want to go in. We all do. But if we send in a team to be caught with Shay and Granger, we need a big enough team on the outside to extract. We only send in the people we *know* they'd expect. Who would that be?"

Reece bristled. If people were going in on his orders, he should be one of the people going in. "It depends on what they know."

"Okay, let's assume they know most of what we know," Cody continued. "Who is on the North Star roster right now that he'd expect to come save Shay?"

Reece hesitated, but honesty was the way to go. He had to remember what it had been like to be an agent and an operative. Emotions couldn't cloud decision-making. "Saunders, Trevino, Lindstrom and Daniels for certain. Parker is iffy. He's been semiretired, but known to show up when the mission is dire."

"That's five with Parker, which leaves us six out here. I say we go for it," Cody said.

"Lindstrom will have to get back with the dog," Tucker pointed out.

"Yeah, let's get a message to Elsie of our plan.

Once Saunders is back, we'll move to reconvene with the other team and go forward."

Reece wanted to argue, but he kept his mouth shut. Sometimes a plan wasn't great, but it was the only chance you had.

And he'd take whatever chances he needed to get Shay and Granger safe. He owed them both that much.

Chapter Fifteen

Shay was tired of being taken off guard, but Frankie had done another one-eighty. While he'd left Granger chained to the wall, he hadn't ended up playing his "game." He'd left the cabin.

Likely to nurse his wounds. That at least made her smile.

She was cuffed, but could walk the room freely. Of course, the armed dude at the door meant she couldn't walk right out, but she could go stand next to where Granger was chained to the wall.

She understood that this in it of itself was a game. *Wait. Wait. Wait.* She was supposed to worry Frankie was off taking down the North Star operatives after her. It was why she'd wanted to do this alone and yet now that the threat was here…

Something about fighting Frankie had recalibrated her mind. Or maybe something about not being in charge. She trusted her team. Yes, it was possible they'd get hurt, but Frankie clearly underestimated them.

Even if he's been watching you for two years?

She couldn't let her mind dwell on *that* question, so she focused on the here and now. "Why is he leaving us together? Practically unguarded?" she muttered to Granger.

"On the inside. I'm sure we're guarded quite well on the outside."

Shay eyed the one guard inside. He was one of the guards who'd let her beat up Frankie. "They didn't exactly jump in to protect their boss, did they?" She spoke quietly, in the hopes the guard wouldn't hear, but the room wasn't all *that* big, so it was possible he heard everything.

Still, he only stood by the door and stared ahead. But Shay had to wonder, if she could get through to one of Frankie's guards...

"I feel like we're missing a piece of something. He wants us to wait around so he can kill our friends in front of us, okay. But then what? How satisfying is *that*?" Shay murmured.

"And what if our friends don't fall into his trap?"

Shay thought of the flashlight. Elsie was supposed to be able to hear everything. Including Frankie's little admission. Would it be enough to keep everyone safe?

She eyed the guard again. What if she could get him on her side? What might they be able to accomplish? She knew Frankie ruled with fear over loyalty.

She glanced at Granger. He too was staring at the guard. When he moved his gaze to hers, he shrugged in what limited capacity he had. "Worth a shot," he offered, apparently his thoughts going in the same direction hers were.

Maybe one guard couldn't get them out of here, but one guard might help them get out of here once things went down. Whenever that was going to be.

"Hey, buddy? When do you think your boss is coming back?" Shay asked, shouting across the room so it couldn't be mistaken that she was talking to him.

The guard shrugged and he didn't look at her. He'd been in here the whole time, but Frankie had left him behind. Was it because he trusted the man inside so much, or the men outside more?

Still, she thought back to when she'd been pounding on Frankie. It had to be clear to anyone with experience that she was way better than Frankie. And still they'd let her pound on him until Frankie had given the order to stop.

"I bet you enjoyed the show," Shay continued. She thought about walking toward him, trying to create a more conspiratorial atmosphere, but she wanted to wait for an in. A sign she might be able to get to this guy. "You've probably wanted to pop him a few times."

The guard's eyes flicked to her briefly. He said nothing and went back to looking at the wall.

But that look was an opening. Shay pushed off the wall and began moving toward him. Slowly, casually. "I've seen the way the guy treats what he calls 'the help.' I wouldn't blame you for not liking him. After all, you're not getting paid to *like* your boss."

She was halfway between Granger and the guard. The guard didn't say anything, but he was watching her now. So, she turned back to Granger. "You know who knew how to treat his men? Frank senior."

"Yeah?" Granger offered with some interest. "I never knew him."

Shay had never met Frankie's grandfather either. He'd been in jail the whole time she'd been with Frankie, but people had talked about Frank Vianni in hushed, awed tones. Not the way they talked about Gio or Frankie. "That guy? He knew how to earn some loyalty."

"Frank was all right, my dad always said," the guard said. He shifted when Shay turned back to face him. He adjusted his gun and he frowned, but he didn't tell her to stop talking.

"Yeah, that older generation, man. They knew how to do it."

This guard was youngish. In his thirties, maybe. Likely this was a family affair for him too. His dad had worked for Frank, maybe Gio. Maybe even Frankie.

"That's what my dad always said," the guard said, nodding slightly. "Didn't like the way the new guard was handling things."

"Who could blame him? Times change, sure. But that doesn't mean you start treating people differently."

The man slid a worried look to the door behind

him. "*You* were *really* with Vianni?" he asked with some interest.

Shay shrugged casually, moving a little closer. "Was, yeah."

He looked at the door again, then to Granger on the wall, then her. "You learn to fight like that there?"

Shay laughed. "Frankie prefers everyone around him to be weaker than him. Even his muscle." She pointed at the gun the guard held. "That can do some damage, sure, but he could afford better for you guys. And that gear you've got." Shay made a dismissive sound. "I'd never equip my team with such a sad excuse for protection."

It was a bit of a reach. The gear the guard wore was perfectly acceptable, if a little bulky and old. But it'd get the job done.

But now the guy looked down at it with some concern, pulling a bit at the bottom of the vest like he was worried it wasn't big enough to protect him in a shoot-out.

He looked at the door again, then took a step toward Shay. The guard leaned his head in, kept his voice low. He still held the gun pointed at her, but she wasn't worried. She didn't want to wrestle it from him or take him out—there were too many like him on the outside—but if she could get him on *her* side, it might come in handy.

"How'd you get out?" he asked, his voice little more than a whisper.

Shay's excitement leaped, but she had to tamp it down. Get too eager, offer too much, and she'd ruin everything. She had to be calm and careful.

But if she could get this guard on her side… The possibilities were endless.

GRANGER DIDN'T MIND watching Shay work. She had an easy way about her that had often allowed her to do just this. Engage, probe without seeming to and convince. It had made her an excellent operative, the way she could blend in and out of a situation. Regardless of the situation.

It helped that she was a beautiful woman, and something about her looks made men a little less leery of her than they should be. Even if they'd just watched what she could do.

The guard was clearly intrigued by the idea she'd been a part of the Vianni family and then gotten out. Likely he was of the belief that if this *woman* could do it, surely he could too.

It was interesting a man this close to Frankie would be entertaining thoughts of getting out. A man whose family had been working for the Vianni family for at least a generation or two.

But that was the problem when you didn't reward loyalty. When you fancied yourselves above the men who'd come before.

Fear did wonders, but if a little awe or loyalty wasn't mixed in, fear didn't win in the end. The earlier generations had been hard to shut down because their men had been afraid *and* loyal.

But Gio and Frankie had done a lot to erode that. Which was why, Granger supposed, Frankie had decided to fake his death and hang out in the wilds of Idaho. If it was possible, he'd be home in Chicago pulling the same old strings, but it wasn't. And not just because he was wanted for all his crimes.

Frankie didn't have the influence there. He needed isolation to build up this team and keep them loyal to him if only because there wasn't much else to do out here.

If they could turn his team against him…

Well, it was something.

Shay stood close to the guard now. Granger could hear their conversation. She offered some complaints about the way Frankie used to treat his men. It took some time, patience, but she eventually got him to share that he'd been overlooked for a lucrative job that he felt he should have gotten. When he'd told Frankie that he'd spent his whole life in service to the Viannis, Frankie had been dismissive of both him *and* his father.

Clearly this man had a lot of resentment for the way his dad had been treated at Frankie's hands, but he felt a generations-old duty to the Viannis. Could Shay get past that?

"Loyalty. Look, I'm no mobster, but I'm no cop either. Sometimes you gotta bend the law, sometimes you get *paid* to do that, but if the guy paying you isn't going to bail you out, then what's it all for?"

"My dad owed a lot to the Viannis."

"The Viannis or Frank? Because Frank ain't here."

The guard nodded almost imperceptibly. He still leaned toward Shay in a confessional sort of way, but he hadn't loosened the grip on his gun. Clearly, he wasn't dumb muscle. He was being careful.

Still, he could be a formidable ally if they could get him to take that step. If *Shay* could get him to take that step.

After a few minutes of silent thinking, the man straightened, shaking his head somewhat regretfully. "Look, Frankie's paying me. More than you could possibly dream."

Shay sighed, but she didn't have anything to fight that with.

But Granger did. "How much do you think I can dream?" he asked.

Both Shay and the guard looked over at him. The guy's face went blank, almost as if he'd forgotten Granger was there and that he was with Shay alone.

"What are you offering?" the guard said shrewdly.

"You help us get out of here? More than Frankie is paying you. I guarantee you that."

The man studied him carefully. "How are you going to prove that you've got the money and will give it to me if I help you?"

"Good question. I'd need your help to prove I've got it, being as that I'm chained up and all. As for getting it after you help us escape, I figure you're a smart enough guy to track me down if I try to flake."

The guard shook his head. "I can't unchain you. I can't…help you guys. I'm just one person. Frankie's got a whole team. I'd love to take the money and run, but it isn't possible."

Granger attempted a shrug. "All I'm saying is, I've got the money. I'd certainly be willing to pay someone who saved my life. Take it or leave it, but the offer is on the table from now until I'm safe and sound." He maintained eye contact with the man. "You don't have to take it now to take it."

The guard didn't respond. Instead, he took a few steps backward to stand right in front of the door again.

Shay smiled a little and walked back to Granger. She arranged herself casually against the wall, then leaned toward him. "I can't tell if you're underestimating how much money Frankie pays, or if you're playing this guy," she whispered.

Granger stared at her. She really didn't know? "I don't think I'm doing either."

She scoffed. "You don't have that kind of money."

"Who says I don't?"

She gaped at him, but the door was opening and there wasn't time to explain to her that he'd always had more than enough money. *Money* was never the issue.

Frankie moved inside, and Granger knew immediately it was bad news for him and Shay. Because Frankie was *beyond* pleased with himself.

"We've got a few of your friends." Frankie smiled broadly. "Now the fun can really begin."

CODY WYATT HAD never once expected to return to the fold of North Star. Doing a few computer things here and there was one thing, but actually going into the field leaving his wife and daughters at home…

He didn't like it. They were his life and he'd left behind all the danger and uncertainty. Happily. Because his wife and girls filled all those holes he'd carried around before them.

And yet he'd come here because he owed his life to Shay a few times over. *And* because his wife had insisted. His wife who had somehow wound up knowing more about Shay than he did. "Veronica," he muttered. "She tells my wife and not me."

"I'd tell your wife a lot of things before I'd tell your hard head," Tucker offered good-naturedly.

Cody scowled at his brother. Though Tucker hadn't worked with Shay as long as Cody had, they'd worked a mission together. A mission in which Shay had purposefully defied Granger Macmillan to help save the woman who would become Tucker's wife.

Tucker had also left behind his wife to help save Shay. Because he owed her too.

They *all* owed her.

Cody eyed Jamison. His stern older brother hadn't asked questions when Cody had explained the situation. Cody had only had to mention Shay, and Jamison had volunteered. He hadn't needed his wife to urge him to do it, but then Jamison and Liza were always on the same page it seemed.

Jamison and Shay hadn't ever worked together, but Shay had been Cody's partner when Cody had stepped in to save Jamison from being killed by their father. Shay had been integral to getting Jamison and Liza and all the girls they'd saved from the Sons of the Badlands to safety.

Two of the girls who Liza and Jamison had then adopted. So, Cody supposed that's why Jamison hadn't needed urging. Shay had helped save the women who would become his family.

The three brothers were standing in the cold, the sun a tiny hint on the horizon. It would be better if they could continue to work with the cover of night, but that wouldn't last too much longer. Still, they had to wait. It would be a few more steps before the Wyatt boys got to wade into the fray.

Reece Montgomery, former North Star operative and de facto leader of their little group tonight, stepped into the clearing where the Wyatts waited.

"Step one is complete," Reece said flatly.

Which meant Vianni men had taken the agents named Zeke Daniels and Mallory Trevino. Connor Lindstrom and Gabriel Saunders would follow in step two.

"I'd feel better with video," Cody said into the silence.

"Wouldn't we all? We can't risk it. Elsie is adamant about that."

Reece was keeping in contact with their head tech, practically a full-time job with the old analogue radios they were using. Cody wished he had access to a computer. He could set up some kind of secure server, and it would enable him to do a lot of things that might give them better eyes and ears on what was going on inside wherever Granger and Shay were.

But it would take time. Elsie was using that time to keep everyone on the same page, and he was using that time to lay a trap with his brothers.

Cody heard the faint tapping, a North Star sign. A few minutes later, another North Star operative appeared. He came to stand next to Reece.

"I laid the explosives," Holden Parker said. "Good for me to go?"

Reece nodded. He looked grim and remote, but when he spoke there was something softer in his voice. "If that's what you want to do."

"I'd rather fight *with* Shay than wring my hands out here," he said, grinning at Reece with an ease that spoke of years working together.

"Be careful," Reece said, both a warning and an evidence that these men had a close relationship.

Because this new North Star under Shay's leadership wasn't like the well-oiled machine Granger's had been. Cody had appreciated Granger's ruthless efficiency, but he thought Shay's building a family might have done a lot more *good*, not just stopping the *bad*.

Cody glanced back at his brothers as Holden Parker disappeared into the trees once more. It would be up to the Wyatts now. Them and Reece. To fight from the outside, while the purposefully trapped operatives worked from the inside.

But it would only work if they could figure out exactly where Shay and Granger were.

And that was proving to be more difficult.

Chapter Sixteen

Shay had to work hard to keep her bravado in the face of Frankie's utter glee. "Sure you did, Frank. I bet all my operatives are right outside." She put all the disdain she could manage in her voice, hoping like hell the fear didn't shine through.

"Oh, don't be silly, Veronica. I'm not going to put you all in the same space so you can outsmart my guards. But I understand your suspicion. After all, you like to lie when it suits you. Why shouldn't I?"

"*I* like to lie?" She shouldn't be offended by a mobster's opinion of her truth telling, but it rankled. *He* was the liar.

"Still, I don't expect you to just believe me. You've always been a suspicious harpy."

"Harpy," she echoed, trying to fight back the wave of anger. Whatever names he called her didn't matter. Why was she letting it matter?

Frankie moved across the room. On the wall directly across from where Granger was chained, there was a drop cloth covering something. Shay had assumed it was furniture, but when Frankie pulled it off, it revealed some monitors.

Her dread increased, but she kept the bored look on her face. Didn't even watch while Frankie fiddled with plugging some things into the wall. Instead, she looked at her boots, at the chains that held Granger to the wall, at the guard who wouldn't meet her gaze.

Eventually, Frankie crossed to her. She held his gaze to prove she wasn't afraid of him, even though it made her stomach roil with the lowering memory that she'd married him. On *purpose*.

"Have a look, Veronica, sweetheart." He reached out and trailed a finger down her cheek, like he used to. She did everything she could to suppress the shudder of revulsion that moved through her. He'd use that against her, and in their current circumstances, she couldn't afford to fight him off.

Luckily, he seemed too proud of himself over this monitor thing. He grabbed her chin. "Don't be difficult, darling." His grip on her face tightened, and he wrenched her head in the direction of the monitors. "I would never lie to *you*," he crooned into her ear, even as his fingers dug into her face.

She rolled her eyes at him and sighed with exaggerated impatience. But she did as he asked and looked at the monitor, ready to pretend to be unmoved. There were a couple black squares on the screen. Only one wasn't black. It showed some kind of room. Not like the one she and Granger were in. This appeared to be more like a basement. She wondered if it was in the compound she'd originally tracked.

But why would Frankie hold her and Granger out in this cabin *away* from that, and keep *her* operatives in his compound? Assuming he actually had them.

Frankie released her abruptly, swearing under his breath and stalking back to the monitors.

Shay moved closer to study the screen. She saw two people standing off to the side. Frankie muttered something into what she assumed was a comm unit and then the angle of the monitor changed. Suddenly she could see four people. Two of Frankie's men holding guns pointed at two of *her* people.

Zeke and Mallory. Mallory Trevino had been on board for two years. They'd picked her up on one of their last raids on the Sons. A fantastic fighter, great with weapons and a tenacity that put most of the other operatives to shame. She was married to another one of her operatives, but they'd both stayed on with North Star.

Shay studied her on the monitor. She didn't look any worse for the wear. No bleeding or bruising. Mallory didn't favor a leg or hold her arm. Granted, she might be pretending to be fine out of pride, but...

What if she wasn't hurt? That would be strange, because even if she'd somehow been taken off guard, Mallory would have fought. Tooth and nail. It would have taken more than one man to take her down, and she would have had to have suffered some injuries in the process. Even a gun to the head wouldn't have stopped her from trying to fight.

Shay turned her attention to Zeke. He was their newest recruit. A cousin of Mallory's who'd proven himself willing to play rookie and do whatever was asked of him without complaint.

He too appeared completely unharmed.

Maybe there were circumstances where Frankie's men could have been clever enough to capture Mallory and Zeke without giving them an opportunity to put up a fight, but Shay couldn't imagine one.

She *could* imagine why her operatives would have been caught without putting up a fight though.

Her mind racing, she looked back at Granger. He was staring at the screen with a pensive look. Did he see what she saw, too?

"Now, the first part of this game is simple," Frankie said cheerfully. "I'm taking my guards with me. You try to escape, your friends die. And I'll make sure you both watch it from here. They try to escape, you two die, and *they* watch. Fun, right?"

He walked over to her again and brought his hands up to her cheeks, framing her face gently.

She thought about head butting him. It would be enjoyable, and she knew the guard wouldn't step in *right* away. But there was something about the look in Frankie's eyes. Different than earlier. Not angry but not reckless either.

No, everything he'd planned was falling into place just the way he wanted. Her blood ran cold.

Something was off. Whatever he wanted… Too many things didn't add up. "Why the games, Frank? Just tell us what you're after. You've got us. Why wouldn't we give it to you?"

Frankie laughed. And laughed. His hands dropped from her face and he laughed all the way to the door.

He turned, his hand on the knob. He clucked his tongue. "I'm almost impressed. You've *finally* realized that *you* are not my end goal. Congratulations." He grinned at her then, a full-on challenge. "But if I told you what my end goal was, you might be able to stop me. And we can't have that, can we, my darling wife?" He chuckled to himself and left.

The guard gave them both an enigmatic look, then he departed too. Apparently part of Frankie's game *was* giving them a means to escape.

Which meant, he didn't want them at all.

Shay stared at the now-closed door, a new wave of dread closing over her. If he didn't want her, or Granger, and they didn't know *what* he was truly after, how were they going to get out of this?

Granger's worst suspicions were confirmed by Frankie's exit. The way none of this added up had been weighing on him, and now he fully understood why.

If Frankie really wanted Shay, he would have hurt them more by now. Maybe killed them. The games were all well and good, but he wasn't really doing *anything* to them.

"What's Frankie playing at?" he asked, hoping Shay had some magical insight. Some theory that could move them forward.

"Psychological warfare?" she suggested, but he could tell by her expression she didn't believe it.

"Maybe, but…" He shook his head. "He could be actually torturing us. Or them. There are so many things he *could* be doing. But he's waiting around. Collecting us. Letting us stick together in pairs. That isn't the smartest move."

"He underestimates us." She said it as though she was trying to convince herself.

"He does, but this is more than that." Granger frowned at the screen. He looked at the two North Star operatives who didn't even look mussed. "They got caught on purpose."

Shay turned her gaze to the screen as well and let out a breath. "Yeah, I think so too. They'd be hurt if they'd fought back. And Mallory's hardly afraid of a gun to her head. She would have fought. Probably would have won too. But even if she'd have somehow lost, she would have the marks of a fight."

Granger nodded, glad Shay backed up his hypothesis.

Her gaze moved to him and she shook her head. "Well, we might not be able to escape just yet, or figure out what Frankie is after, but we can at least get you out of those."

"How?"

She looked around the cabin, then rooted around

in corners and cabinets. A few moments later, she returned with a tiny screwdriver and a fork.

Granger raised his eyebrows. "Really?"

"You have no idea what I can do with a screwdriver and a fork," she replied, smiling at him. Clearly wanting him to laugh.

He couldn't quite manage it. Too much was at stake. He'd thought he'd understood what Frankie was after, but it was clearly something else.

Frankie had been watching them for two years. Why had he acted *now*? He was happy to mess with all of them, but wasn't intent on actually harming them. Even when he'd dragged Granger outside, all he'd done was say a few things to try and hurt him.

Frankie enjoyed casual cruelties like some people ordered a milkshake. He'd take the chance when he had it, but it clearly wasn't his goal. Their misery.

So what was?

When the first chain fell, a relief he hadn't expected coursed through him mixed with the surprise Shay had managed to get it off the wall. It was uncomfortable to be tethered to a wall, but also left him with a demoralizing feeling of being utterly helpless while everyone around him wasn't.

She silently moved over to the next one. The chain was still on his wrist—she'd only managed to get the whole chain out of the wall, not off his wrists, but he didn't care if he had to spend the next few weeks with the shackles hanging off his wrists. At least he could *move* and wasn't chained to a wall.

When the second one fell, his center of gravity went a little wonky. Like his arms suddenly weighed twice as much as his body. His back to the wall, he slid to the ground, his butt hitting the hard floor with a thud. "I'm fine," he said automatically. "Just felt like sitting."

She snorted, looking down at him from where she stood. "Yeah right. Dizzy?"

"I'm fine."

"Your head is not fine," she said, eyeing the wound on his head. "It's not *actively* bleeding, but no doubt you need stitches, food, water, rest." She touched his hair, just above the wound, tentatively. But it felt like a caress.

And that was something he couldn't think too much on. Especially since it brought to mind the kiss they'd shared and that was…well, hardly the point right now. "I'll get them eventually. How's your side?"

"Fine enough."

"Which is why you're bleeding through your shirt."

She looked down at her shirt and wrinkled her nose. "Might have popped a few stitches kicking his butt."

Granger finally managed a laugh. "On a scale of one to ten, how satisfying was it?"

"A million," she replied emphatically, which made him chuckle again.

It hurt his head, but there was something freeing about being able to laugh, no matter how dire a situation they were in. "On the plus side, those two didn't get caught on purpose just for fun. There's a plan in place."

Shay nodded. "We probably shouldn't say too much." She nodded to the monitors. "Who knows who's listening." She lowered herself next to him, so they sat hip to hip. Her body heat seeping into him and hopefully vice versa. She was tired from digging him out. Tired from all of this.

"Rest," he ordered.

She eyed him. "And what are you going to do?"

"Play human pillow until you wake up or someone comes back."

"We can't just wait around."

"I think we have to for right now. Until we figure out what he's after. He's cocky. He'll slip up eventually." He kept his voice low. It was possible Frankie had the whole cabin bugged, but also possible no one was listening. They needed to communicate. If they did it in whispers, the risk had to be worth it.

Shay seemed to think over Frankie's inevitable slip, but as she did she gingerly rested her head on his shoulder.

Granger moved his arm around her shoulders, gratified when she leaned into him. Something eased inside of him when she did. Not just grateful that she'd lean, but comforted by the contact.

"He wants them to come after us. So he can kill them in front of us. In front of *me*. That's what he said."

"But when you asked him what he wanted just now, he said he wouldn't tell because we *could* stop him. You couldn't stop him if he wanted to kill Mallory. He could just go in and shoot her. Or have one of his men do it."

Shay's eyebrows drew together and she slowly lifted her head off his shoulder. Something like loss moved through him.

"I guess that's…true," she agreed carefully.

"And he didn't say he'd kill them in front of anyone exactly. What were his exact words?" Granger tried to remember precisely the way Frankie had said it.

"He said, 'you will watch everyone you love die,'" Shay said flatly.

His arm held her a little tighter, brought her a little closer. Now that they were in this position he couldn't stop himself from offering her comfort. Too close. Too many things to think about.

"Watch everyone you love die. That's a lot of people. If he wants us all to die in front of you, why are we separate? Why not toss us in the same place and blow us up?"

She pulled away from him just a hair, staring at him with something like horror crossing her features. His arm was still around her, but she'd leaned away a little.

Granger realized that he'd sort of suggested *she* loved *him* in some way. He cleared his throat, suddenly uncomfortable, and shifted on the hard, cold floor. Then he started to pull his arm away, but stopped himself.

He hadn't meant *love* love, and she knew that. Or should.

Unless…she *did* have those feelings for him.

Chapter Seventeen

Shay desperately wanted to stand, to get away from all…*this*. They didn't have time for it, and she realized—too late, clearly—when he'd said *loved* he just meant in the same way she loved all of her North Star family.

Not that he surmised she'd been in love with him for far too long. Her secret shame.

But he was smart and quick and she had the terrible sinking feeling that he was probably putting it together as they sat there.

Granger moved his arm, like he was about to pull it away, and then he seemed to think better of it. He leaned closer to her slightly turning his body so he could look her right in the eye. From the expression on his face, she knew he'd compartmentalized it all away.

Once again he was thinking of the mission.

Just like old times, she thought with some bitterness, even though she knew it was the right thing to do in the moment.

"He's luring everyone here," Granger said, excitement making his whispers just a shade louder. "To kill them in front of you. Okay, sure, it's revenge, but Frankie would need something to be in it for *him*. He could have gotten revenge on you anytime in the past two years it seems. What's in it for him on top of the personal satisfaction of watching you suffer?"

Shay looked away from him. To concentrate, she had to. She stared at the wall and willed the embarrassment heating her cheeks away. "I can't begin to imagine. If I could…" She frowned a little as she trailed off. *Luring everyone here.* She knew North Star would follow, but she thought they'd send a team. She looked back at Granger. "Everyone. Is *everyone* here?"

"No, not everyone. I think there were some concerns about information leaking. Elsie pulled together the team members she trusted implicitly."

"Everyone important to me." She leaned closer to him again, keeping her voice a quiet whisper in the short distance between their faces. A theory began to form, one that made her heart beat hard, and oddly enough, hope spring warmly in the pit of her stomach. "Everyone we can trust. Here. Which means no one we trust is back at headquarters, at least in Elsie's estimation right now. We know Frankie knows the location of headquarters, and if we have every senior North Star member here, headquarters is easily infiltrated."

Shock slammed through his expression. "He could

be after some kind of information. If he was working with Ross Industries, or any of the other groups we've taken down in the past few months, he could want the information in Elsie's computers. He's been watching for two years and still hasn't been able to get what he wanted or needed."

Shay didn't argue at his use of the word *we*. They didn't have time for her to point out she'd had to drag him into missions kicking and screaming before this one. She'd remind him of that later. "And if he wants that information, we're superfluous. *This* is a game. A distraction."

"And he can kill us all when it's over, but for now, he just needs the chance to get in and get that intel. And he might need one of us to get it. Or he wants to use what he finds against us. If he wanted us dead, we would be dead. So, this isn't about us. Not now. Not yet." He leaned his head toward the flashlight. "Elsie, do you hear me? We need people at headquarters. Not here. Headquarters."

Elsie couldn't respond to tell them she'd heard them. Or communicate that she understood. They just had to hope she was listening. And that she didn't send anyone else to be captured by Frankie.

Because apparently that was *exactly* what Frankie wanted, even if they fought their way back out again.

"She'll get it communicated to everyone," Granger said, and she wanted to be reassured by his certainty. It *exuded* from him. His tone of voice, the way he held himself.

And she realized, in a way she hadn't before, that it was an act. He wasn't sure. He wasn't certain at all. How could he be?

When you were a leader, you pretended. He was faking, so they could move forward with the mission regardless of any uncertainty. He'd *always* been pretending. Every mission. Every order. And…

"You never told me," she said hoarsely, feeling unaccountably emotional. "You threw me into the deep end and you never told me it was all an act."

He had the audacity to frown as if confused. "What was an act?"

"The bravado. The knowing everything." She moved away from him, out of the comforting weight of his arm. More than anything, she wished she could look at him without the pain in her eyes, but she knew he'd see it. She couldn't *hide* that. "I thought something was wrong with me that I didn't always know the right thing to do, or if a decision I made would work out. You made me think I *had* to have absolute certainty, and I always felt less because I didn't."

Shay got to her feet because she knew this wasn't the time to hash this out. Hell, what they *should* be doing was trying to escape. Trying to get to headquarters themselves. They were *operatives*. They had done riskier things, fought off bigger threats.

So what in the world were they doing sitting here talking about the past? About her *feelings*? Why was she even bringing it up?

"I'm sorry," he said. And he sounded like he meant it, which somehow infuriated her even more.

"You're *sorry*?"

"You're right. I didn't…tutor you in the way I could have. I didn't plan to…" He got up himself, and she had to bite her tongue to keep from telling him to be careful. She had to curl her hands into fists to stop from reaching out to make sure he was okay.

Because no matter how angry she was, how many old hurts were swimming to the surface, she didn't want to see him in pain. Weakened. *Again.*

She'd been afraid, despite all her efforts to pull him out of that burning building, he was going to die. And he hadn't. But a part of him had. He'd been in a wheelchair. Had sequestered himself away. He'd cut them all off for a time and…

"I'll admit, I didn't handle passing the baton very well," he said gravely. "I never planned to pass anything. North Star was mine. It wasn't really, but I needed to think it was. Back then, it was my revenge and I guarded it ferociously. I didn't see it that way at the time, but the past two years…" He let out a sigh. A heavy sigh born of loss and change and understanding.

Shay found suddenly she wanted none of it. Fear threatened to swallow her whole. She didn't want Granger's truth or his honesty. "This isn't what's important," she said, trying desperately to convince herself.

"Maybe not, but I have a feeling we'll never talk

about if we don't have it out now. We're alone, Shay. Maybe someone's listening, but what does it matter if Frankie hears our issues?"

"What does it matter if we never talk about it?"

A muscle ticked in his jaw. "Maybe you plan on dying here, but I don't," he said, and where he'd sounded tired before, he only sounded angry now. Angry and still so certain.

It's an act. It's an act. But it was hard to believe that when his gaze held hers so fierce and determined.

"Neither of us are dying here," he said, an order that brooked no argument. "I plan on walking out of this and having a future, and I want you in it."

GRANGER HADN'T PRECISELY meant to say that. It was a truth he'd been turning over in his head for a while now, but he also understood that he couldn't crash into Shay's life with his own epiphanies. He'd kept his distance for a reason, and allowing her to make her own choices was one of them.

Or at least, he'd convinced himself it was one of them. Maybe it was his own cowardice.

But now she'd opened that door, and he could have let her shut it. Like they'd both done in the past. But that's not what he wanted. Not anymore. They'd played this game for too long, and it was time to put an end to it.

"Hold a gaze too long then look away. Pretend it

isn't there. We've done plenty of that. For a while it was necessary, but it isn't anymore."

"Pretend *what* isn't there?" she asked, but her voice was hoarse and her eyes were wide with something he so rarely saw on her. Fear. He should have some sympathy, some patience, but he didn't. Not with his head throbbing and his emotions churning.

"Do you really want to play dumb, Shay? It doesn't suit you."

"And I suppose you know what would?" She crossed her arms over her chest with a mocking look. "Tell me, Great Granger Macmillan, what would suit me?"

"You think I don't understand you? That I don't see through you picking a fight so you don't have to deal with the actual *emotion* here."

She looked away, pretending to scoff, but the fact that she'd broken eye contact told him everything he needed to know. Because no matter how little she *wanted* to deal with her emotions, they were all at the surface.

Shay felt betrayed by him. By the way he'd left her in charge. And he'd realized he'd done it badly, but he hadn't realized she'd struggled so much. Internally, clearly, because no one who followed her, him included, had guessed.

He stepped toward her, and she eyed him warily. He could tell she wanted to step away, but her pride wouldn't let her. She lifted her chin.

"So, I am sorry. You're right. I didn't do the things

I should have done. I didn't know how, and I was so wrapped up in my own failures I didn't think... I only knew you could handle it. And you have. No matter how you've felt, you have run North Star as well, if not better, than I did. You know that. The team you've built, the fact some of them have left to build actual *lives*, it's a testament to the leader you are, no matter *how* you feel about it."

Her jaw worked, her eyes suspiciously shiny, but she didn't lower her crossed arms and she didn't acknowledge any of those words.

"I wish I could have done things differently, but in the moment, I didn't know how."

"You almost died," she said, her voice barely more than a whisper. It wasn't absolution exactly, but it was close.

Except... "You made sure that didn't happen." He reached out and touched her face. Which had him thinking about that kiss back between the rocks. She'd initiated that, and before that moment he'd convinced himself that whatever Shay felt for him was a little residual hero worship. He'd saved her once, under far better circumstances than she'd saved him from not so long ago.

But she'd kissed him like they were equals. She'd kissed him in the *moment*, and he hadn't thought about the past. He'd only thought about her and now, and he had to believe she was in the same boat.

Or she would have been disappointed. Unaffected.

She was neither. Then. Now. He bent his mouth to hers, but she pulled back.

She stepped away from him, something very young and vulnerable on her face for only a second before she schooled it away. "You're attracted to me. Sure. You want us to be honest about that? Fine. There's attraction on both sides."

He laughed, and maybe it shouldn't be quite *that* bitter, but he knew what it was to…go down this road. It was hard and it required a raw, soul-deep honesty he truthfully hadn't been quite ready for when he'd married Anna.

But he had to remind himself that Shay had never loved and lost, she might have built a family with North Star, but her first experience with a romantic relationship was the childish choice she'd made with Frankie, and ever since then her only relationships had been within North Star. They might have shaped her, helped her gain confidence and strength, but even old hurts could make smart, strong women unsure.

So he tried to keep his voice gentle. "If it was about attraction, and only that, it wouldn't be so damn fraught, would it? It wouldn't require this dance we've been doing for *years*."

At the word *years*, her gaze jerked back to his. She swallowed unsteadily. "You loved your wife."

"I did. But she isn't here. And that took some time to…accept. To work through and figure out what that meant. I love a lot of people, Shay. When they die that love doesn't die with them, and love sure as hell isn't finite. I don't only have a cup of it to dole out. It might be easier if I did, but that's not the way the world works."

Every time he said the word *love*, she took another step back. As if carefully retreating from an angry bear. "Why are we talking about this?" she asked, and she looked at him with such *hope* that he'd sweep it under the rug. That he'd close the door they always closed.

But he didn't want to anymore. He took all those steps she'd retreated. He wanted to reach out and touch her, but he thought maybe she'd listen better if he delivered it like an order. Like a mission.

It was *his* mission.

"I am in love with you, Veronica. Shay. Whatever you want to be called. Whatever you want to do. Fight. Hide. Lead. Follow. It doesn't matter, it hasn't *mattered*, because I am in love with the person you are. And yes, I needed time away from you and North Star to figure it out, but it was *inexorable*. This feeling."

She looked *horrified*, and he wanted to laugh, honestly. Leave it to him to fall in love with a woman who'd be horrified by a confession as honest as that.

He held her gaze, unafraid of his own vulnerable feelings. He'd loved and lost before. It was nothing he wanted to experience again, but as long as she stayed alive… Well, the rest didn't matter so much.

She looked away, and said nothing. She held herself so still like she believed if she was still and quiet enough he'd forget. Pretend it never happened.

But whatever she was staring at made her eyebrows furrow, and then her eyes widen. She pointed at the monitors on the opposite wall behind him. "A second room just appeared on the screen."

Chapter Eighteen

Shay's arm shook. It was inexcusable, because no matter what Granger had said that might have pierced her very soul, a second box on the monitor had clicked on and she had a bad feeling that meant another North Star member had been apprehended by Frankie's team.

On purpose or not?

I am in love with you.

It couldn't be. *He* couldn't be.

She lurched forward when Holden came on the screen. "No."

Granger turned around to see what she saw, and followed as she crossed the room. She wanted to punch the screen. Three of her operatives, in separate cellar-like rooms. She was shaking her head without understanding. "Why did you do this, Granger? They'd all be safe if you hadn't done this." She knew it wasn't fair to blame him, but fear from this and fear from everything Granger had said to her was making her irrational.

"He's unhurt. Look at him," Granger said in her ear before he gave her a little shake with one hand. "He meant to get caught."

"Idiot. That stupid, moronic, idiotic *fool*." She swore a few times to make herself feel better. "He's supposed to be retired. He's supposed to be in Nebraska on that little farm with Willa and raising cows or some stupid thing."

But she said *stupid thing* and a longing she didn't understand welled up in her. She found Reece's choices baffling. A bed-and-breakfast? With people coming and going? A ready-made kid—no matter how cute Henry was, Shay didn't know how he dealt with the emotional minefield *that* had to be.

But Holden's life… Well, there was something about his wife's little farm that had seemed charming. Downright…homey. No matter that Shay knew nothing about farms or animals, she'd been a little jealous.

And hadn't understood that any more than she understood Granger being in love with her.

I am in love with you.

He'd said it with such conviction, like it was his one and only truth.

"You know a ranch isn't all that different from a farm," Granger said. "Mine's still small, but I have plans to expand. I always wanted to be a cowboy when I was a kid."

She turned to stare at him. Had he read her thoughts? Was he…offering something?

He shrugged, looking back at the screen. "If you like that sort of thing."

She could not make sense of him. Of this. They were *prisoners* of a man who, technically, might still be her husband, since they'd both only faked their deaths. And that man was likely trying to get some kind of sensitive information from North Star headquarters and Granger was talking love and ranches.

"We have to survive this," she said, meaning to sound like a scolding schoolteacher, but it just came out kind of breathless.

Granger nodded. "Yes, we do. So, why not have something a little extra to survive for?"

She blinked, unable to fully take it on board. Any of it. "That head wound has done a number on you, Macmillan," she muttered and turned her gaze back to Holden on the screen.

He looked as brazen as ever. Lazily leaning against a wall, grinning at someone out of sight with that sharp-eyed glint she knew meant he was trying to rile them up.

"Why are they getting caught on purpose?" Shay muttered, studying the screens as if they could tell her. Mallory and Zeke sat in a corner of the room they were in. They looked relaxed and unbothered.

Granger took her by the arm, and God help her the way her heart leaped at his big hand curling around her arm was a *problem*.

But she shoved the feeling away as he pulled her over to the cabin corner farthest from the monitors.

He took her hand, gentle. *I am in love with you.* It echoed in her head, over and over, in that same calm, serious tone. Like he knew exactly what he was saying. Like he had no doubts.

He gave her palm three quick taps. And she realized he wasn't holding her hand to hold her hand. This was no offer of comfort or support or *love.* He was going to communicate with her through taps like they did in the field sometimes.

She nodded, signaling she was ready for him to start, and she forced herself to focus on the taps of his thumb against her palm and what they signified instead of the feel of his other fingers holding the top of her hand in place.

They have three. Still nine out there, plus Betty and Elsie. Divide and conquer.

It made sense. Get more operatives on the inside, keep some on the outside, then you have two distinct fronts. Except those on the inside were locked up and without any access to weapons. They'd have to rely on some kind of diversion.

Diversion. Her head whipped back to Holden on the screen. She pressed Granger's thumb out of the way with her own, a sign it was her turn to tap. Then she gave him one simple word. *Explosives.*

Granger considered, then nodded.

Holden was an explosives expert. He would have, hopefully, known where to lay some before he got caught. If he had some kind of detonator to set them off, he would and it would be diversion enough to fight their way out.

Then what?

She inhaled deeply and slowly let it out. Granger had gotten her all...out of sorts. She couldn't think clearly and it was all his fault.

Shay looked down. He was still holding her hand. Their fingers intertwined. Gently. Carefully. Perfectly.

Shay felt like she had in the moment she'd stood in front of all of North Star while Granger explained he wouldn't be back and that she would take over. He was reordering her world and she wasn't *ready*.

But she didn't pull her hand away.

GRANGER REALIZED HE was actually holding his breath. Everything felt so tenuous, Shay's hand in his most of all.

So he didn't breathe and he didn't move. He just let his mind turn over all the information they had. Because though he'd learned a thing about how dangerous it could be to compartmentalize, sometimes it was necessary. Sometimes it was life or death.

Holden had clearly gotten himself caught before Elsie had been able to relay his message about headquarters being the real target. He *had* to believe Elsie was listening. That she *could* get the information to everyone.

But what if she'd missed it? He released his breath and leaned his mouth to his flashlight. All the while keeping Shay's hand in his. "Elsie, if you're listening, it's imperative to get everyone off this site and get them to headquarters. Stop whatever is going on at headquarters," he repeated in a low tone. "Vianni might have heard this, so make sure everyone is watching their backs."

Shay blew out a breath, shaking her head. "We should do something."

He understood she felt useless and frustrated, sitting here, playing prisoner. He felt it too, but he also knew that sometimes a plan took patience. "Like what?"

She held his gaze, as if searching his eyes for something very specific. Her fingers twitched in his, but he didn't let her go. "If we try to escape, we could stop anyone else from getting captured," she said. But it was with a note of hopefulness, because she already knew the pointlessness of that plan.

"And leave Zeke, Mallory and Holden behind?" He used the tapping to communicate again, not wanting to risk anyone knowing who was still out there. *Still eight out there. Give Holden time.*

She shook her head again, not in disagreement but in annoyance. Because she knew the answers. She knew what they needed to do—she just didn't *like* it. But this was Shay, and for her, hope sprang eternal. She never fully gave up.

It was one of the many things that had added up to make him fall in love with her, when he wasn't looking, when he was desperately trying not to. All that trying not to seemed so silly now.

He used his free hand to cup her cheek. His thumb brushed across her cheekbone. She was pale. They likely both were. They'd been beat up pretty good with minimal food and water and sleep between leaving and now. She was still recovering.

But they'd survived physical wounds time and time again. It was the emotional ones that seemed so hard.

However, she held his gaze, and she didn't pull her face or hand away. It was like the moment in the rocks, when she'd kissed him, except there was a lot more wariness on her face now. He had a feeling the word *love* had put it there.

Color had crept into her cheeks, and her breathing was far more shallow than it had been. He didn't doubt she had *some* feelings for him, even if she didn't express them. But he wasn't sure what she felt was…the same.

And he knew, he'd never have the opportunity to get through to her like this. In real life, she'd disappear, throw herself into a mission, bar him.

No you won't let her do that. That was a bone-deep conviction. He wouldn't let her disappear, but he also knew how to seize a moment when it was presented to him, no matter how ill-timed.

"I know you're attracted to me, and I know you care about me." She jerked under both hands, but he held her still. Trapped—unless she wanted to fight

him off, which God knew she could. "I know there
are some tangled past feelings mixed up between us.
But I know what I feel for you in the here and now
isn't about the past. The man I am now is not the man
I was then and—"

"Yes, you are. You're the same *man*, Granger," she
said softly, gently, as if it wasn't a slap. "You simply
started understanding yourself now."

He opened his mouth to deny it, but no sound
came out. "I made…mistakes. *You* pointed out many
of them. I lost myself and—"

"I understood what you were doing. It's why I
called you out. Not because you were irredeemable,
but because I knew it was a road you'd regret going
down. Because you weren't that guy, no matter how
hard you tried to be. I've always seen *you*. Even when
you didn't see yourself."

It was some kind of absolution he hadn't known
he was still looking for. Relief and comfort. Even if
he wasn't sure he believed it.

"We've both changed, sure," Shay continued, looking fierce and certain. "We grew up. We dealt with
our losses and our blows. People…grow. But you're
not a different man and I'm not a different woman."

"So what are you saying then?"

"Just that…" She looked down at their joined
hands, her eyebrows drawn together. He'd seen her
fight off gangs of men and take bullets and stab
wounds with equal aplomb. She wasn't afraid of
anything.

Except this.

She exhaled, her breath fluttering across his cheek.

Blue eyes. Intelligent and scared. He let his thumb drag against her cheek again and her breath caught. She shook her head, vaguely, not a refusal so much as a rebuttal to some inner thought she was having.

But then she leaned forward and pressed her mouth to his. Again. It was gentle, and careful, and he let it stay that way. Let her set the tone, the pace. Let her make the choice.

He wanted *her* to make the choice that would make *her* happy. She pulled away, but not fully. Just her mouth from his mouth, and she exhaled unsteadily. Then she leaned her forehead to his chest, almost like surrender. "I've loved you for far too long, even when I desperately, definitively, didn't want to. Including this moment."

He slid his hand over her messy braid. If that was supposed to hurt his feelings, she misjudged how much he wanted her to love him. "I'll take it."

She let out a huff of breath, something very *close* to a laugh, but before he could say anything or she could, the door flew open with a loud bang.

They both jumped, not coming apart in guilt as much as surprise and an innate readiness when a threat dawned. Though both now stood in a crouch, ready to fight off an invasion.

Operatives to the last.

Frankie stood frozen in the doorway, studying them. As if he'd seen it all. Or heard it all. But no, he looked faintly confused, so Granger didn't think he'd heard or seen anything. Nothing specific.

But he certainly…suspected something. His eyes were too narrow, his gaze too discerning.

"We have another one of your friends," he said, suspicion still all over his face. "This one was a bit of a surprise, I have to say. I didn't think you'd have *old* operatives coming to your rescue. But maybe the new set aren't quite so loyal." He closed the door and strode over to the monitors and tapped the one that showed Holden.

The kiss and emotion finally drained away enough that Granger got it though to his brain he should stand or sit, no longer crouch ridiculously waiting for an attack that wouldn't come.

Yet.

Shay straightened at the same time he did, like they'd recovered and come to the same conclusion simultaneously. Frankie looked back at them, still that odd puzzlement on his face. Almost a…detachment.

Oh, he obviously wanted to mess with them, but this wasn't *about* them. It became clearer with every interaction.

Granger looked at the screen where Holden still stood, casually and cheerfully. If Holden had laid explosives. If he was waiting for the right time to set them off and create that diversion—

The door opened again and the guard Shay had talked to earlier stepped in. "Boss?"

"This better be important," Frankie barked, not bothering to look away from the monitors.

The guard looked at Granger and Shay, an inscrutable look on his face. He walked over to Frankie. "Peretti found this on the prisoner." He held out a tiny black box. "Some kind of detonator."

Granger's hope congealed, turning to acid as the detonator was passed to Frankie.

There would be no diversion.

Chapter Nineteen

The disappointment was like a knife to the heart, when Shay's heart was way too exposed as it was.

Holden's plan wasn't going to work. No diversion. The plan was shot.

She should be working toward a plan B. They all should be, but her brain was scrambled.

Why did she keep *kissing* Granger? And why had she admitted she *loved* him? But the shock on his face when she'd said he was the same man he'd always been had undone her.

He always did. So why was she fighting it when he wasn't?

She looked at Frankie warily, to find him examining her. He was a cunning man, and a strangely insightful one when he wanted to be. When he wasn't busy obsessing over himself. He could, on occasion, read people when he wanted to manipulate them.

He wanted to manipulate her, both related and unrelated to what he wanted. Revenge. His goal. There was something at headquarters he wanted.

It explained the siege a while back. He'd found out their location, found a way to get them all out of the way, but then the men he'd sent had bungled it all.

Or *had* they? Frankie had been watching them for two years he said, somehow having done something back after the explosion. But he hadn't moved until *now*. Something had changed. He'd accessed *something* when she'd been shot.

He looked away from her and back at the monitor, and she surmised he understood that she too could read him, even when he could read her. Even ground.

"Your friend was going to try to blow us up," Frankie said as if working through the information. "Clever," he admitted with a nod toward the monitor. "Except the part where he kept the detonator on his person. I don't think someone planning on getting caught would do that." He turned to her again, all easy smiles. "Do you?"

Shay didn't let her reaction show. He was making it clear Holden hadn't gotten caught on purpose, but…

She refrained from looking at the monitor while Frankie was studying her, but she thought about what she'd seen. Holden's causal demeanor. He was an excellent actor and could charm just about anyone.

But some of his skills had dimmed after *falling in love*. When he'd suddenly had someone to live for and come home to.

Wasn't that why she was so deathly afraid of her own feelings? Reece had left. Cold turkey. And it was like he *had* become a different man, though she understood fundamentally he hadn't. He'd just kept his real self better hidden than anyone she'd ever known.

She didn't want that kind of transformation. It terrified her.

Holden hadn't cut everything off as Reece had, but he wasn't quite as good at his job anymore.

She was going to lose Elsie and Betty all because they'd found men to *love*, all because they'd found something outside of North Star to set their sights on.

They had all *changed*, not who they were but what they wanted and what they valued and Shay couldn't bear to go through that again. She'd done the whole metamorphosis once. It was hard. It was painful. It led to confusion and loss and she didn't *want* it.

Of course, if she lost today to Frankie, she was going to lose North Star altogether. Possibly her life and those she loved. *That* was a little scarier than change.

Not the losing North Star so much. *That* didn't terrify her the way it should have. The way it once had. It almost…almost felt like a relief.

She snuck a glance at Granger. It wouldn't feel that way for him. Or some of her younger operatives. What would Sabrina do? *She* hadn't changed for love. She'd been severely slowed down by almost dying and all, but she hadn't…

Okay, she had changed. Not in any obvious ways. Not in any *big* ways. It was more in her awareness. Like Holden. She was more careful. Kinder.

She had someone to come home to. She had been given a softness and an understanding she didn't quite know what to do with, but it had become enough of her that she returned it in a way she hadn't before.

Shay had watched love make some of the people she cared for above all else in this world *better* people.

And none of that would matter if they all didn't find a way out of this without anyone getting hurt.

Shay knew that meant she had to act. Not because she was frustrated and tired and strung far too tight, but because it was time. North Star had men on the inside, men on the outside. Likely Elsie knew headquarters was the target since Granger had relayed that information twice now.

It was time for all hell to break loose for Frankie.

So, she moved toward him. She gave Granger a look. *Stay exactly where you are*, she willed him. He watched her, and she could see the careful wheels in his head turn. He gave her an imperceptible nod.

He understood what she was going to do. And, thankfully, he approved.

Shay couldn't let out a breath of relief though. She had to keep herself calm and casual. So she kept her eyes on Frankie, not the detonator in his hand. If he turned to look at her, study her, she would stop and stare at Holden and allow herself to worry.

Because that's what Frankie wanted from her, and

for now she'd give it to him. If she could get to the detonator.

She didn't look back at the guard. She'd trust Granger to give her some kind of sign if he started paying too close of attention.

She inched across the room. Frankie noticed but didn't tell her to stop. She pretended to be horrified and unable to look away from the monitors. Moving close like she could save them through the screens.

When she was close enough Frankie was in reach, she gave one brief look back at Granger. He'd moved, but closer to the door. He was chatting casually with the guard. Keeping the guard's focus split so he could fight him off if something occurred.

She'd take Frankie. He'd take the guard.

Perfect.

Shay was *this* close to reaching out and getting her hands on that device. She considered grabbing it and running. But Frankie had a gun on Granger, one hand curled around the handle, because he sensed her being perhaps a little too close.

If she *was* just a diversion, he might kill her in a fit of pique before she could both push the detonator *and* stop him. So she stopped where she was.

Frankie held the detonator cupped in his hand. All she had to do was reach out and slap the button on the detonator. All she had to do was be faster than him and use the chaos that ensued to make her move.

He glanced at her, and she quickly moved her gaze to the monitor. Holden was standing there, looking like he didn't have a care in the world. He looked like he might actually be *whistling*. She wanted to laugh, but instead closed her eyes and let out a sigh like she was in pain.

Then, quick as lightning, she reached out and slapped the detonator. She couldn't tell if she'd managed to press the button because she had clearly taken Frankie off guard. The small black box clattered to the ground.

Shay quickly, *carefully* put her boot on it, depressing the button for sure this time, without crushing the device.

Nothing happened.

They all looked at each other in shock. No booms. No shaking of the ground. Absolutely no indication any explosives had gone off anywhere near them.

Frankie said something into what she assumed was his comm unit. His scowl deepened. He shoved Shay out of the way and picked up the detonator, then studied it, fury crawling into his features. He threw the detonator at the guard. "Have Peretti check this out. Is it a decoy?"

The guard nodded and immediately disappeared.

Frankie's hand was still curled around the handle of his gun and Shay watched, mind scrambling, as he decided what to do.

He *wanted* to kill her. She could tell that. But he didn't.

"That was very stupid, Veronica," he said, his voice sharp and razor-thin. A man on a tightrope.

Shay shrugged. "It was worth a shot."

Frankie pulled in a slow, measured breath. He looked at the monitors, then, slowly enough to have Shay's stomach curdling, his gaze turned to Granger.

"You'll come with me, Macmillan," Frankie said, sounding overly formal.

Shay nearly reached out to keep Granger right where he was. It would have been a grave mistake and she just narrowly kept her arms at her sides.

Frankie smiled at her like he knew exactly what she'd been thinking. "I think Veronica needs to learn her lesson." He took Granger by the arm and opened the door. He yelled at one of the guards outside to come in. "Make sure monitor three is on," he said to the guard when he stepped inside, and then roughly jerked Granger out of the cabin.

GRANGER'S MIND WHIRLED trying to make out what had just happened. He wasn't so worried about Frankie. Not yet. He was keeping them alive for a reason.

Frankie had clearly *wanted* to kill Shay right there. His hand had twitched on that gun with a fury that even Granger had to admit was ruthlessly pounded back.

Why hadn't Holden's explosives worked. Had it just been a threat? A trick? If so, for what purpose?

Frankie's hand was like a vice. Granger thought about fighting it off, but the man wasn't stupid. They were only alone for a moment or two before three guards appeared.

He transferred Granger to the guards, one on either side with a firm grip on either arm and one behind pushing a gun into his back.

Granger wasn't concerned for himself just yet. He'd survived worse. As they propelled him forward, he took the time to notice the world around him. He'd lost track of time inside the little cabin. The way the sun slanted through the trees he could only guess it was getting toward afternoon. He didn't study the surroundings for too long, too afraid he might see a North Star operative and give them away.

Granger considered his chances of fighting the three guards off. The head wound held him back a little bit, that and not having any weapons. Still, he'd fought off more men on his own before. What was his record? Five or six?

Three, well four, wouldn't be impossible, but Frankie hanging back made it risky. The mobster would have backup, or his own gun to shoot Granger with if he felt like it.

Maybe he'd get more information and insight from Frankie if he went along with whatever this was. More intel to pass along to Elsie to prevent whatever was going on at headquarters. *If* she was still listening.

So, he was lead by all these guards on a long march. It must have taken an hour at least. The sun had moved that far. Granger had to admit he was feeling a little woozy. Head wound. Lack of food, water and sleep. The piercing, bitter cold.

Once upon a time he'd been trained for this, but the last two years had been more about recovering from his injuries and enjoying ranch work, not so much building himself back into a man who could withstand this kind of torture.

He thought of Shay, holding herself back when Frankie had grabbed him.

For her sake, he'd withstand a lot no matter the circumstances, even if it took sheer force of will.

They began to approach some buildings, and Granger had to wonder if this could be the compound they'd originally mapped. Was this where Holden, Mallory and Zeke were? Maybe he'd have a chance to rendezvous with all of them.

Was Frankie that stupid?

Granger eyed him as the guards pushed him into a doorway. Inside was a cold cement room that looked an awful lot like the ones on the monitor back in the cabin.

Frankie followed him inside, but the guards stayed outside. One hovering in the doorway, but the other two quickly dispersing.

Granger had to smile. He could definitely take two of them.

"These are your new accommodations, Macmillan. Don't worry, you won't be staying here long."

"You marched me all this way just to kill me? Sounds like a lot of extra work for nothing."

"Except here they'll never be able to find your

body and pin it on me," Frankie said with a smile that had Granger's nerves beginning to hum.

He might be able to take Frankie and his guard but they *were* well armed.

Granger studied Frankie standing there, looking smug and superior. He just needed to get under his skin. Like Shay had.

"Why don't we settle this just the two of us, Vianni. Man to man," he said, nodding at Frankie's gun. "Show your team here you aren't a coward."

Frankie's nostrils flared and his hands curled into fists, but Granger couldn't quite get him going the way Shay could.

When Frankie spoke, his voice was cold and controlled. "I let Shay do that. I'm not stupid. I suppose you've done an admirable job improving the muscles of your little operatives, but I much prefer to use my brain."

"Whatever you gotta tell yourself after your exwife beats you up."

"She's *still* my wife, Granger. You might do well to remember that."

Granger snorted. "Sure, I'm really worried about it. Your marriage and your *brain* that got you so far in life. What with hiding away in a cabin in Idaho rather than living the high life in Chicago."

Frankie's hands uncurled from fists. The sparking anger seemed to cool. "I'll get my life back," he said. Calmly.

Granger laughed, trying to make it caustic enough

to reignite the other man's anger so he made a mistake. "Yeah, sure."

But Frankie simply shrugged out of his jacket, and then pulled his gun out to examine it. "I would have done this in front of her, but she'd get in the way. Probably try to save you. Foolish girl that she is. So, this will have to do. Her watching from afar." He pointed at a camera bolted to the wall above. Then he used the gun to point at Granger. "Take off the vest," he ordered.

And that's when Granger realized that Frankie might still want Shay alive for some reason, but him on the other hand?

Not so much.

Chapter Twenty

Shay watched the monitors, nerves strung so tight she could barely breathe. She knew she should be searching for a way to escape, trying to get some kind of message to North Star or *something*.

But she kept watching to see if Granger's face would appear on the screen.

"It's going to be a while."

She whirled around. Released a breath. She hadn't noticed the guards had switched because she'd been too absorbed with willing Granger's face to appear. The man from before was back. The friendlier guard.

She marched over to him. The only thing that kept her from grabbing him by the vest and shaking him, demanding help, was the way his grip tightened around his gun.

She stayed where she was, just a little beyond arm's reach from him, and narrowly resisted clasping her hands together and getting on her knees to beg. Plead. At this point, she'd do whatever it took to get to Granger.

Because there was something about the way Frankie had led him away that gave her the horrible feeling she'd never seen Granger again.

"Help us," she implored. She looked at the guard, letting every emotion show on her face even knowing it was unlikely he'd be moved by an emotional plea. He'd probably killed men. He worked for a mobster for heaven's sake, but she'd do anything. *Anything.*

"Look, lady, there isn't anything I can do." He almost sounded apologetic. Or she was just that desperate to believe she had a chance.

But Shay decided to grab on to that faint apology for dear life. "Granger said he can pay you more than Frankie is." She inched a little forward.

"Yeah, but everyone would have to get out alive for that to happen." The guard shrugged. "Chances of that aren't great for your guy. Look, I feel for ya and all, but I'm not risking my neck."

Another inch, a careful inch, as her heart pounded so hard in her ears she could scarcely hear. She held the guard's gaze. *Look at my face. Look at my face.* "Just let me go," she cajoled. "That's all you have to do. Not save me. Not help me. Just let me walk out that door."

He scoffed.

Keep your eyes on my eyes.

"Come on," he said. "I'd just wind up dead."

"Okay, let me go, and you run too." She did everything she could to make it sound conspiratorial instead of desperate. "We both just run. If Frankie's preoccupied with Macmillan he won't know for a while."

"You can't pay me. *He* was the one with the money," the guard said, jerking his chin toward the door Granger had been pulled out of only ten minutes or so ago.

Shay swallowed at the bile that wanted to rise in her throat. She didn't have time for fear, and she certainly had to entertain every possibility, if only to get out of *here*. "If Macmillan is dead, I'll get his money. You can count on it."

There was a pause. She moved another inch and then another. He glanced down at her feet and Shay froze, holding in her last inhale.

"You'll probably just kill me instead of pay me," the man said skeptically. He adjusted his gun, not quite pointing at her, but closer. So he'd only have to lift it an inch or so to do some damage.

"We aren't Frankie," Shay said, with bone-deep conviction as she kept looking at his face, willing him to look up at her. "We aren't the Viannis."

He was frowning at her feet, noticing how close she was. How close she'd moved. She hoped to God he chalked it up to her pleas and not to what she was about to do.

"Please," Shay said, letting her voice shake, letting all the fear she felt make that word tremble like the desperate begging it wasn't.

He looked up at her again. "I ca—"

She'd gotten close enough she could finally act.

She elbowed him in the throat first, and then immediately grabbed his gun. He had more than one on him, so a struggle ensued. She had to get them all. She had to run.

She had to get to Granger.

Shay didn't want to hurt the guy. He'd at least *entertained* kindness, even if he hadn't been able to follow through.

But this was Granger's life on the line, and that made her a lot less empathetic.

She kicked one gun away, but he managed to get an arm around her neck. Clearly she'd blown any chance of getting him on her side. She lifted a leg and got a good kick into a vulnerable place. He didn't go down but his arm loosened enough she could whirl and punch.

Gut, chin, throat.

The guard gasped for a breath, but he still didn't go down. He reached for the gun holstered on his leg so Shay lunged for it too.

She swept out a kick meant to take him down, but he swiveled enough for it to do the damage.

He was a *much* better fighter than Frankie, or any of the other men she'd come across on her way here. No wonder he was guarding her.

Still, none of that mattered. She had to get to Granger. She'd do anything, use any skills she'd honed, to make that happen.

He landed a knee that made her legs buckle, but she fought tooth and nail to remain upright. She feinted a kick and then instead spun around with an elbow. It landed with a sickening crack against his nose.

The guard let out a grunt of pain as blood spurted and Shay used the momentary surprise to knock him over. He landed with an *oof* on his stomach and she jumped on top, using a knee in his back to keep him down while she quickly divested him of all his weapons and tossed them to the far end of the room.

She was still wearing her vest so she pulled some zip ties she always kept in one of the pockets and began to restrain him.

"You really think you're going to get away?" he asked, sounding bitter and resigned.

"I'm going to try." She gave him a friendly pat on the shoulder as she studied her handiwork. He was still on his stomach, hands tied behind his back, ankles tied together. He might be able to get upright or crawl out to the other guards.

But she'd be long gone by then.

She stood, breathing heavily. She felt a bit woozy and her gunshot wound pulsed with pain, but she couldn't hold on to any of those feelings because her brain just kept thinking: *Granger, Granger, Granger.*

The other guards could be coming for her. She should be more surreptitious, more careful. *Don't do something stupid or you can't get to Granger.*

She took a deep breath and slowly, carefully edged the door open. Looked around. She saw white. Trees. No one else.

Shay slid outside. In the distance, standing in a small circle were a group of guards. It almost looked like they were standing around a campfire, and it was directly where the footsteps—Frankie's and Granger's—led.

She moved around the back of the cabin. In front of her was nothing but trees, and she didn't spot anyone. There *was* a camera pointed at the place she would need to go, but unless that camera came with a gun, she wasn't worried.

She'd move into these trees, then with enough distance, head east. As long as the footprints led in that direction the whole way, she'd be able to pick up the trail a ways out.

If not, Granger had the flashlight radio to Elsie. He wasn't totally alone. If she couldn't get to him, someone would.

Someone *had* to.

She made a run for the woods, zigzagging through trees just in case, and trying to keep as quiet as possible.

When someone silently stepped out from behind the tree she was just about to dart around, she barely swallowed back a scream. *Gabriel.*

He grabbed her arm and Connor also appeared, Froggy at his side.

"Luckily Froggy led us to you just in time, huh?" Connor said, already moving forward, in the same direction Shay had been going.

Gabriel was pulling her along.

She wanted to crumple in relief and exhaustion, but there was no time. "Granger?"

"Wyatts and Reece are on him," Gabriel said as they quickly moved through the trees.

There wasn't a group she trusted more. But she trusted herself the most. "Can you get us there?"

Gabriel shared a look with Connor. Connor nodded.

"We can get you there. We've got a Jeep a ways out. They walked, so it'll be worth the time added. If we run."

"What about—" Shay gestured at the guards who were starting to realize something was amiss. One spotted them and pointed and yelled.

Gabriel held up a little device, that looked suspiciously like the one Frankie'd had earlier. "This'll keep them busy. Other one was a decoy."

Shay let out a breath. The danger wasn't over, but something inside of her loosened. She could fight for Granger's life. For her own. "Then let's go," Shay said, already moving into a full-on run.

The explosion sounded behind them before the first gunshot.

GRANGER STEELED HIMSELF for the gunshot, so the burst of static had him flinching. But it was no gunshot.

It was Frankie's comm unit. There was a frantic murmur of voices. Frankie put the earpiece in his ear, and his frown turned into a thunderous scowl.

Granger couldn't hear any of the words. But

Frankie's were clear. "She what? How long? An *hour*?" Frankie whirled away from Granger and stalked away. He kept his voice low, but Granger caught little snatches of words. Sentences.

"Don't say another word until you've got her in custody. If you have to kill her, so damn be it."

She'd escaped. Maybe that guard had helped her or maybe she'd just managed all on her own. Granger laughed, big and booming no matter how it hurt his head. How could he *not* laugh?

Shaking his head in awe, he supposed this was part of why he loved her. She'd always managed to make what seemed impossible *possible*. Here she was, doing it again. "She got away," he said, more to himself than Frankie.

Frankie lifted the gun again. "All the more reason to kill *you*."

"Yeah, I guess." Granger shook his head, but it didn't matter. Shay had escaped, and that was all she'd needed. Frankie's men wouldn't capture her now. Not with North Star out there lying in wait.

"Why are you smiling?" Frankie demanded. His finger hovered over the trigger and Granger *knew* there wasn't much chance he got out of this alive. Frankie would kill him out of spite if nothing else. Right now the man was shaking with rage, but he was clearly trying to get his temper under control.

It would probably be best if Granger let him without poking at him. It might prolong his life. Give North Star agents a chance to get here.

But he couldn't stop himself. It just struck him as all too funny. "You're going to kill me and then what?"

"None of your business."

"What do you get out of it? Satisfaction? For what? A few minutes? An hour? It doesn't last. So what's the point?"

"There is no point in killing you. You're right. You mean nothing, and I am killing you as nothing more than a momentary pleasure—a mix of revenge, hurting Veronica and hating your guts. But it would be *beneath* me if that's all I was after. You built your beautiful North Star for good, but now it will be mine and it will do terrible things and make me very, very rich."

It shocked Granger, and maybe Frankie as well. The cold self-satisfaction melted off his face as he seemed to realize he'd explained his plan to Granger.

His sneer widened and he shoved the gun into Granger's chest.

Granger couldn't be sure Elsie would have heard all that. So, he repeated it as succinctly as possible. "You don't even want information. You want to impersonate us."

"No, I will use all your processes, contacts and resources and the good name you've built to destroy. Not just the thing you built, but anything that suits me." He was scrambling to justify telling Granger his plan, trying to make it sound like it was something he was doing *to* Granger.

But in the end, all Frankie really wanted was North Star, and maybe it was age or time or just knowing that life was unpredictable and dealt blows you didn't expect, but it didn't hurt the way it might have once upon a time.

"Thank you for telling me that, Frank. Really." He knew that he'd likely die. No one was coming to save him, but even with the vest off, the flashlight was right there and Elsie had to have heard that.

So she could stop Frankie. She could stop North Star from being used for its opposite purpose.

He had some regret over dying, over not getting that shot with Shay. Regret it had taken him this long to take the chance.

But at least he wasn't going out without having stopped something.

"I'm going to kill you," Frankie said, making a point of shoving that gun barrel into his chest even harder. "North Star will be mine. I'll ruin everything you were, and I will stop Shay. She will be my prisoner for the rest of her miserable life. I want you to know that before you die. Just because I can, I will ruin everything you are and were."

Granger shook his head, looked Frankie right in the eye. If he was going to die, he was damn well going to do it with his head held high. "No, Frankie, you won't."

But the last word was drowned out by the loud echoing sound of a gunshot.

Chapter Twenty-One

They ran and as far as Shay could tell, no one followed. The explosion had worked at keeping the guards busy or injured or unable to get through the blast's aftereffects to follow.

"What about Holden, Mallory and Zeke?" Shay asked breathlessly.

"They're being held closer to where Granger is. Before Holden allowed himself to get caught, he set some explosives strategically where it would allow them to get out. It was all connected to the same detonator, so they should be escaping their rooms right now and meeting up with the Wyatts and Reece," Gabriel explained.

He pointed up ahead where a Jeep came into view. They didn't slow their speed, simply jumped in. Gabriel took off with a speed that should have scared her, what with the fact they had to dodge trees and boulders.

But she couldn't entertain fear. She was too busy

mouthing prayers to keep Granger safe. To keep her *family* safe.

Gabriel drove like a bat out of hell, God bless him, and when he skidded to a halt, they were all jumping out simultaneously with the jerk of the car being thrown into Park.

Connor and Gabriel began to run, so Shay followed. A strange calm had come over her. She was with her operatives. They were going to save Granger. Things were going to be okay.

Because she willed it. Because she would do whatever it took.

They wouldn't come this far only to lose Granger. She simply wouldn't allow it.

But she came up short in surprise when she saw Sabrina standing next to Reece. "What on God's green earth are you doing here?"

Sabrina grinned. "Good to see you too, boss. Had to bring out the dog," she said, jutting her chin at Connor and Froggy behind her. "Don't worry, I've kept away from the fighting fields."

She didn't have time to scold Sabrina, so she'd make sure to remember to do it later. Shay turned her attention to Reece who stood with his arms crossed surveying Cody who was laid out with a large rifle, balanced on a rock. He had his eye on a scope and his fingers around the trigger.

"Holden is out, he's helping Mal and Zeke take down the rest of the guards, so I sent the other Wyatts and Nate to make sure they're all good. Which works, because it took the guard who was stationed out here away," Reece explained, as if not at all surprised to see them.

Still when she got close enough, he clapped her on the shoulder. A quiet *glad you're okay*. She swallowed at the lump of fear and emotion in her throat and gave Reece a faint nod.

Shay looked out over where the gun was pointed. They were high up on a ridge, below a small valley with a collection of buildings spread out.

"Mal and Zeke are in that far one," Reece said, pointing out to a squat building far off in the distance. She could just barely see specks of people. She had no doubt her team would take down Frankie's guards.

"Granger's in this one," Reece said pointing to the small one closest to the ridge. *This* was the compound she'd discovered in the beginning, but Frankie must have known that. That's why he'd used the other cabin, to try and cause confusion. To be able to separate them, not just in these small buildings, but by location.

And it didn't work, you little bastard, did it?

But it wasn't done yet.

"Once the guard was gone, we could see this little window," Reece continued to explain. "More of a slot really, likely to pass things through or let some natural light in."

"I've got Frankie," Cody said, his eyes on the sight. "You're not supposed to be able to see through the window, it's some special glass or plastic, but I've got a special sight that sees through it. I can take him out with one shot."

Take him out. It would be over. Frankie would be dead. She looked at Cody's finger curled around the trigger.

No. "You can shoot, but don't kill him," Shay said.

Cody looked up from the sight. "Isn't that a risk?"

Shay shook her head and then gave Cody a nudge so he moved out of the way. She took over. Laid out like he'd been, looking through the sight.

"He's not going to die a noble death," Shay said, adjusting the gun and her finger around the trigger. "He's not going to be some gangster myth. I trust Granger to do what needs to be done once we immobilize Frankie. That bastard is going to waste away in prison just like his father. And *that* will eat him alive." She watched through the sight, as Frankie shoved the gun into Granger's chest.

Then took her shot without qualm.

GRANGER KEPT WAITING for the pain to slam through him. He could hear the gunshot. The echo of it. But nothing hurt. He was still on his feet, didn't fall, and there was no sudden blow of pain after the shock wore off.

He was standing. He was fine.

Frankie wasn't. He was writhing on the ground, holding his right wrist. Blood pooled underneath it.

The gun had fallen out of his hand and lay on the floor, forgotten.

As if in slow motion, Granger looked around the room. There was a small rectangular window on the door, giving off light. There had been plastic or glass there, but it was broken now.

He'd been saved.

He didn't know how they'd managed, but they had. His knees nearly gave out as he looked down at Frankie, the shot still echoing in his head.

Frankie was moving. Not writhing in pain anymore. No, with his left hand he was reaching for the gun that had been shot out of his hand.

Granger quickly stepped on Frankie's left wrist to stop his attempt to grasp the gun. He exerted a crushing pressure that had Frankie's grip on the gun loosening and caused a blood-curdling scream to emanate from his mouth.

The door burst open and Shay and Cody ran in. Cody immediately went for the gun on the floor, while keeping his gun trained on Frankie.

Shay launched herself at him and he narrowly caught her without falling over. "It had to be the two of you," he muttered, holding on to Shay for dear life.

"Your best operatives of all time? Of course," Cody offered with a grin. "But Shay took the shot."

He clearly said that for Frankie's benefit. And that had her grip on him easing as she turned to look at the man sprawled on the ground looking downright apoplectic.

But he didn't have any recourse now. Reece and Gabriel entered and between the three of the men, they grabbed Frankie by the arms and got him to his feet.

"Betty's nearby. We'll bring her down to start checking everyone out. She'll bandage him up before the feds get here."

Shay took a step away from him, to stand in front of Frankie.

"Any last words before you're thrown in jail, just like Daddy dearest?"

He tried to spit on her but she dodged it with a grin. "Mature, Frank. Real mature."

"We'll take him out," Reece said. He nodded at Cody and Gabriel, a clear sign they should all clear out and leave Shay and Granger alone.

In the room, absent of any noise, and Frankie's blood on the floor between them, they surveyed each other. He supposed she was doing the same to him as he was doing to her: studying for any sign of new injury, any chance this was a dream.

"So, you saved my life. Again."

"Bad habit," she said, her voice hoarse. "Granger…" She trailed off, like she didn't know what to say.

He didn't either. What words were there? He'd been determined to live, but the last half hour or so he hadn't been so sure *he'd* make it. And now he had. Because of her.

Maybe it should humble him, but he could only

count himself lucky he'd offered a hand that long ago night back in Chicago.

So, no, there weren't words. There was only moving toward her, kissing her and holding on for dear life.

Because now that's what they had.

She held on just as tight, kissed him back just as fiercely. Until someone clearing their throat interrupted.

Slowly, hating to do it, he pulled away. And glared at the interruption.

A grinning Betty, with a bag likely full of all sorts of torture tools to clean and stitch them up.

"Hate to break this up and all," Betty said, biting back a grin. "Like *really* hate to, because if you're kissing, I've just won a very old bet with Elsie she likely doesn't remember, but the two of you need some serious medical attention."

Betty moved in briskly, instructing them both to sit down. She checked out Shay first, clucking over her gunshot wound not yet healed, and the bumps and bruises. She let Shay go, shooing her out of the room, then turned to him.

Betty swore and muttered to him about stitches and staples and concussion protocol. He only listened with half an ear so he could occasionally say yes ma'am at the appropriate moment. Otherwise he stared at that small window, broken, as sunset filtered through.

He was alive. Shay was alive.

They'd won.

People came in and out to update him while Betty stitched him up. The federal agencies that had responded had cleared out. The Wyatts had gone home, though not before Shay and Granger had both thanked them both.

When he was finally released from Betty's evil clutches, his head hurt worse than before. Though she'd given him a pain pill that *should* start kicking in.

He looked at her. She'd stitched him up more than once, also had a hand in saving his life a few times. "Thanks, Bet. I sure hope that's the last time we meet like this."

She grinned at him. "Me too," she agreed.

They stepped outside into a quickly cooling night. Someone had started a little campfire, and almost everyone was standing or sitting around it. Shay was seated, flanked by Reece and Holden. Connor and Sabrina were standing, Froggy lying in between them. Elsie was pacing slightly outside of the circle under the watchful eye of her boyfriend.

His family. Who'd all come together. To help each other, save each other. Do right when there was wrong. Something expanded in his chest, an overwhelming pride and awe—a humbling one.

He hadn't set out to build this. They'd made his revenge into something beautiful. Meaningful. But he'd at least kind of set it into motion.

With Betty, he joined the group of people.

"Well, now that we're all here," Elsie muttered, coming to stand in the middle of the circle. She wrung her hands together, her eyes darting from person to person until they landed on Granger himself. "Um, I have to tell you all something."

"Sounds like bad news, Els. I think we've had enough of that," Holden said teasingly, smiling gently at her.

She didn't smile back. "I know. I'm sorry, but… It has to be done." She bit her lip, looking around at all their faces again. But when she began to speak, she once more looked at Granger directly. "I did something when I heard what Frankie was planning." Nate Averly had come to stand behind her and rubbed his hand up and down her back and she smiled gratefully at him.

Love, clear as day. Granger let out a breath. When he'd started North Star, the goal had been what had happened here today. Putting an end to the evil that had hurt his wife.

But what he hadn't counted on, planned on, what he still wasn't sure how it had happened, was all this *love*.

"When we started figuring out Frankie infiltrated our stuff somehow, that his target was more North Star than any one person, I started…putting together a…a…well, I guess you'd call it a doomsday device."

Granger blinked, suddenly not thinking so much about love. "Doomsday," he echoed.

"It erased…everything. Any trace of us…ever."

Elsie swallowed. "I wanted to wait for your okay, but he was going to kill you and…" She took a deep, shaky breath. "None of you exist anymore, unless you had identities not tied to North Star like I did. I—I even got rid of North Star's money."

Granger's jaw dropped at that. "How?"

"Charities. Foster organizations. Women's shelters. Anywhere that might have taken in a victim of Vianni or the Sons." She moved forward, looking at him specifically with a pleading in her eyes. "If Frankie could do it—infiltrate us, figure us out—someone else could too. It was only a matter of time. And someone else would have had the same idea. I couldn't stand the thought of North Star being used for bad when everything we did was for *good*."

Granger didn't fully know how to absorb this information, but the trepidation on Elsie's face told him…

Well, it told him everything he needed to know. He walked over to her and took her by the shoulders, looked into her shiny eyes. "Elsie, you did it exactly right. You saved us. Not just North Star, but all of us." He gave her a fatherly hug, because God she made him feel old.

Then he turned to face them all. The family he'd collected. The family Shay had made from that. "All of you had a part in this."

"There's one last step." Elsie held up a small detonator like the one Holden had made a decoy of. "Blow up headquarters. Any last chance people figure us out. Holden said the blast will burn everything down, and it can be done without causing damage to anyone or any other properties. I just have to push this button."

There were nods around the fire. Encouraging. Understanding.

"People won't have a place to live if I set this off," Elsie said, looking apologetically at Sabrina, Connor and Froggy and then Mallory and Gabriel.

"We've got plenty of room at the B and B," Reece replied. "We'll take in whoever needs it until people find a place."

"We've got room at the farm," Holden agreed. "Same goes."

"And I've got room at my ranch. Long term," Granger said.

They all nodded. Firm agreement, even if not *happy* agreement. Because this was change, and leaping into the unknown. Back to that real world they'd all escaped, but he searched all their faces and knew they were all on the same page.

This was the right thing to do.

Elsie handed him the device and he stared at it. This would put an end to North Star. To everything he'd built.

But the man who'd built North Star had...changed. Maybe he wasn't a different man like Shay had said, but he had *changed*. Matured. Begun to understand himself.

He pushed the button, and they all said their goodbyes to North Star. Quietly, they sat around the fire. In couples. In groups. Leaning on each other. Watching the fire and ruminating.

Because North Star had brought them all together, and now it was gone.

Shay slid her hand into his and he looked over at her and smiled. It was strange. Sad, even, but good too. He squeezed her hand, a silent *I'm okay.*

Because he was. They all were.

Sabrina cleared her throat. "Con and I have talked about… You know, someday when we were too old for North Star or whatever, starting a search and rescue operation." She shrugged restlessly. "We'd need more than just the two of us to do it."

Connor took Sabrina's hand in his. "Pilots. Trackers. People willing to train the dogs. Money's going to be a bit of an issue but—"

"I wouldn't count on money being an issue," Granger interrupted.

"He's loaded apparently," Shay offered.

"North Star S&R?" Sabrina said with the quirk of her mouth.

"No. It'd need a new name," Granger insisted.

"Why?" Elsie asked. "North Star was a good one."

"I named North Star that because it was going to be my…center. My everything. S&R or any job won't be my guiding light anymore. It shouldn't be any of yours. It'll be a job, and a good one. Maybe even a legacy, but not your guiding principle."

Shay leaned her head on his shoulder. Everyone looked at each other.

"It should be something simple," Betty suggested.

Shay lifted her head up off his shoulder. "Well, we just blew ourselves up to start over, so why not Phoenix?"

The heads around the fire nodded, and it seemed just right. A rising from the ashes. A new start without losing each other. A new venture, using their skills to help people.

Just like they'd always done.

After a while, they finally began to disperse, some people going with Reece to the Bluebird Inn. Others headed with Holden to his farm. A few people, Shay included, heading to his ranch.

He got everyone settled at his rather ramshackle house. Likely they could work together to make the accommodations a little nicer. But Shay wasn't in his room where he'd left her. He had to search the house, then step into the dead of night to find her sitting on the stairs of his porch, each of his dogs on either side of her.

He scooted Ripken out of the way, though the dog wiggled into his lap with a happy tail-thumping glee.

"You going to sleep? Betty says it's rather important and blah, blah, blah."

"We'll sleep soon enough," she returned.

He looked up at the brilliant blanket of stars above. He liked the *we*.

"I just kept thinking over what you said around the fire. You said it wouldn't be your guiding light."

He was looking at it even now, that bright, guiding light. The star he'd looked to too many times to count. Since he was a boy. But it had come to mean something else.

Just like the woman beside him.

"So what will be?" she asked.

He thought that over, still staring at the North Star above. "This ranch," he said. "My own sense of right and wrong." He turned his gaze from the stars above to her sitting next to him. "You."

He held out his hand and she looked at it for a moment. She knew what he was offering. Not just a place to stay, but from here on out, love.

And a lifetime together.

She let out a breath and slid her hand into his. "I guess that works."

"You guess?" He scoffed. "You've been in love with me for *years*."

She chuckled and leaned her head onto his shoulder. "I do love you."

"I love you too," he murmured, and kissed the top of her head, and they watched the stars for a while.

And spent the rest of their lives together.

* * * * *

WE HOPE YOU ENJOYED
THIS BOOK FROM

⊞ HARLEQUIN

INTRIGUE

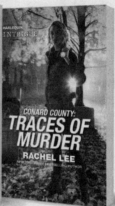

Seek thrills. Solve crimes. Justice served.

Dive into action-packed stories that will keep you
on the edge of your seat. Solve the crime
and deliver justice at all costs.

6 NEW BOOKS AVAILABLE EVERY MONTH!

#2079 SHERIFF IN THE SADDLE
The Law in Lubbock County • by Delores Fossen
The town wants her to arrest her former boyfriend, bad boy Cullen Brodie, for a murder on his ranch—but Sheriff Leigh Mercer has no evidence and refuses. The search for the killer draws them passionately close again...and into relentless danger. Not only could Leigh lose her job for not collaring Brodie...but they could both lose their lives.

#2080 ALPHA TRACKER
K-9s on Patrol • by Cindi Myers
After lawman Dillon Diaz spent one incredible weekend with the mysterious Roslyn Kern, he's shocked to encounter her months later when he's assigned to rescue an injured hiker in the mountains. Now, battling a fiery blaze and an escaped fugitive, it's up to Dillon and his K-9, Bentley, to protect long-lost Rosie—and Dillon's unborn child.

#2081 EYEWITNESS MAN AND WIFE
A Ree and Quint Novel • by Barb Han
Relentless ATF agent Quint Casey won't let his best lead die with a murdered perp. He and his undercover wife, Agent Ree Sheppard, must secretly home in on a powerful weapons kingpin. But their undeniable attraction is breaking too many rules for them to play this mission safe—or guarantee their survival...

#2082 CLOSING IN ON THE COWBOY
Kings of Coyote Creek • by Carla Cassidy
Rancher Johnny King thought he'd moved on since Chelsea Black broke their engagement and shattered his heart. But with his emotions still raw following his father's murder, Chelsea's return to town and vulnerability touches Johnny's heart. And when a mysterious stalker threatens Chelsea's life, protecting her means risking his heart again for the woman who abandoned him.

#2083 RETRACING THE INVESTIGATION
The Saving Kelby Creek Series • by Tyler Anne Snell
When Sheriff Jones Murphy rescues his daughter and her teacher, the widower is surprised to encounter Cassandra West again—and there's no mistaking she's pregnant. Now someone wants her dead for unleashing a secret that stunned their town. And though his heart is closed, Jones's sense of duty isn't letting anyone hurt what is his.

#2084 CANYON CRIME SCENE
The Lost Girls • by Carol Ericson
Cade Larson needs LAPD fingerprint expert Lori Del Valle's help tracking down his troubled sister. And when fingerprints link Cade's sister to another missing woman—and a potentially nefarious treatment center—Lori volunteers to go undercover. Will their dangerous plan bring a predator to justice or tragically end their reunion?

"CHELSEA, WHAT'S GOING ON?" Johnny clutched his cell
phone to his ear and at the same time he sat up and turned
on the lamp on his nightstand.

"That man…that man is here. He tried to b-break in."
The words came amid sobs. "He…he was at my back
d-door and breaking the gl-glass to get in."

"Hang up and call Lane," he instructed as he got out
of bed.

"I…already called, but n-nobody is here yet."

Johnny could hear the abject terror in her voice, and an
icy fear shot through him. "Where are you now?"

"I'm in the kitchen."

"Get to the bathroom and lock yourself in. Do you hear me? Lock yourself in the bathroom, and I'll be there as quickly as I can," he instructed.

"Please hurry. I don't know where he is now, and I'm so scared."

"Just get to the bathroom. Lock the door and don't open it for anyone but me or the police." He hung up and quickly dressed. He then strapped on his gun and left his cabin. Any residual sleepiness he might have felt was instantly gone, replaced by a sharp edge of tension that tightened his chest.

Don't miss
Closing in on the Cowboy *by Carla Cassidy,*
available July 2022 wherever
Harlequin Intrigue books and ebooks are sold.

Harlequin.com

Get 4 FREE REWARDS!

We'll send you 2 FREE Books plus 2 FREE Mystery Gifts.

FREE Value Over **$20**

Both the **Harlequin Intrigue®** and **Harlequin® Romantic Suspense** series feature compelling novels filled with heart-racing action-packed romance that will keep you on the edge of your seat.